DOC SAVAGE'S AMAZING CREW

William Harper Littlejohn, the bespectacled scientist who was the world's greatest living expert on geology and archaeology.

Colonel John Renwick, "Renny," his favorite sport was pounding his massive fists through heavy, paneled doors.

Lieutenant Colonel Andrew Blodgett Mayfair, "Monk," only a few inches over five feet tall, and yet over 260 pounds. His brutish exterior concealed the mind of a great scientist.

Major Thomas J. Roberts, "Long Tom," was the physical weakling of the crowd, but a genius at electricity.

Brigadier General Theodore Marley Brooks, slender and waspy, he was never without his ominous, black sword cane.

WITH THEIR LEADER, THEY WOULD GO ANYWHERE, FIGHT ANYONE, DARE EVERYTHING—SEEKING EXCITEMENT AND PERILOUS ADVENTURE!

About Doc Savage:

DOC SAVAGE: HIS APOCALYPTIC LIFE
by Philip José Farmer

THE SECRET
IN THE SKY

A DOC SAVAGE ADVENTURE

BY KENNETH ROBESON

BANTAM BOOKS · TORONTO · NEW YORK · LONDON

THE SECRET IN THE SKY
A Bantam Book / published by arrangement with
The Condé Nast Publications Inc.

PRINTING HISTORY
Originally published in DOC SAVAGE MAGAZINE May 1935
Bantam edition / November 1967
2nd printing ... October 1968   3rd printing .... August 1969
4th printing .... August 1977

ISBN 0-553-11322-4

Published simultaneously in the United States and Canada

PRINTED IN THE UNITED STATES OF AMERICA

THE SECRET IN THE SKY

Chapter 1

THE FRIEND WHO DIED

THE matter of Willard Spanner was almost unbelievable. It was too preposterous. The newspapers publishing the story were certain a mistake had been made somewhere. True, this was the Twentieth Century, the age of marvels. But—then——

At exactly noon, the telephone buzzer whirred in Doc Savage's New York skyscraper headquarters. Noon, straight up, Eastern Standard Time.

The buzzer whirred three times, with lengthy pauses between *whirs*, which allowed time for any one present to have answered. Then an automatic answering device, an ingenious arrangement of dictaphone voice recorder and phonographic speaker—a creation of Doc Savage's scientific skill—was cut in automatically. The phonograph record turned under the needle and sent words over the telephone wire.

"This is a mechanical robot speaking from Doc Savage's headquarters and advising you that Doc Savage is not present, but that any message you care to speak will be recorded on a dictaphone and will come to Doc Savage's attention later," spoke the mechanical contrivance. "You may proceed with whatever you wish to say, if anything."

"Doc!" gasped a voice, which had that strange quality lent by long-distance telephonic amplifiers. "This is Willard Spanner! I am in San Francisco. I have just learned something too horrible for me to believe!"

Several violent grunts came over the wire. There were thumps. Glass seemed to break at the San Francisco end. Then came silence, followed by a *click* as the receiver was placed on the hook at the San Francisco terminus of the wire.

The mechanical device in Doc Savage's New York office ran on for some moments, and a stamp clock automatically recorded the exact time of the message on a paper roll; then

1

the apparatus stopped and set itself for another call, should one come.

The time recorded was two minutes past twelve, noon.

Thirty minutes later, approximately, the newspaper press association wires hummed with the story of the mysterious seizure of Willard Kipring Parker Spanner in San Francisco. Willard Kipring Parker Spanner was a nabob, a somebody, a big shot. Anything unusual that happened to him was big news.

The newspapers did not know the half of it. The biggest was yet to come.

Financially, Willard Kipring Parker Spanner did not amount to much. A post-mortem examination of his assets showed less than five thousand dollars, an insignificant sum for a man who was known over most of the world.

Willard Kipring Parker Spanner called himself simply, "a guy who likes to fiddle around with microscopes." It was said that he knew as much about disease germs, and methods of combating them, as any living man. He had won one Nobel prize. He was less than thirty years old. Scientists and physicians who knew him considered him a genius.

When Willard Spanner was found dead, many a scientist and physician actually shed tears, realizing what the world had lost.

When Willard Spanner was found dead, the newspapers began to have fits. And with good reason.

For Willard Spanner's body was found on a New York street—less than three hours after he had been seized in San Francisco! Seized in Frisco at noon, Eastern Standard Time. Dead in New York at ten minutes to three, Eastern Standard Time.

A NEWSBOY with a freckled face was first to convey the news to Doc Savage. The newsboy was also cross-eyed. Neither the newsboy, nor his freckles, nor his crossed eyes had other connection with the affair, except that the lad's reaction when he sighted Doc Savage was typical of the effect which the bronze man had on people.

The boy's mouth went roundly open with a kind of amazement when he first saw the bronze giant; then, as he sold the paper, his demeanor was awed and very near worshipful.

"I know you, mister," he said in a small voice. "You're Doc Savage! I've seen your picture in the newspapers."

Doc Savage studied the boy as he paid for the paper. He seemed particularly interested in the crossed eyes.

"Wear glasses?" he asked. He had a remarkable voice; it seemed filled with a great, controlled power.

"Sure," said the newsboy, "They give me headaches."

Doc Savage produced a small business card. The card was not white, but bronze, and the printing—his name only was on it—was in a slightly darker bronze.

"If I asked you to do something," he queried, "would you do it?"

"Betcha boots!" replied the newsboy.

Doc Savage wrote a name and address on the card and said, "Go see that man," then walked on, leaving the boy puzzled.

The name and address the bronze man had written was that of an eye specialist whose particular forte was afflictions such as the boy had.

More than one gaze followed Doc Savage along the street, for he was a giant of bronze with a face that was remarkable in its regularity of feature and a body that was a thing of incredible muscular development. His eyes attracted no little attention, too. They were like pools of flake-gold, stirred into continuous motion by some invisible force.

He read the newspaper headlines, the galleys of type beneath, but there was nothing on his features to show that he was perusing anything of importance.

The skyscraper which housed his headquarters was, in size and architecture, probably the most impressive in New York City. A private high-speed elevator lifted him to the eighty-sixth floor. He passed through a door that was plain, except for a name in small bronze letters:

CLARK SAVAGE, Jr.

The reception room inside had large windows, deep leather chairs, a strange and rich inlaid table of great size, and an impressive safe.

An automatic pistol lay on the floor. A pig, a shote with long legs and ears like boat sails, walked around and around the gun, grunting in a displeased way.

A man sat in a chair. He was a very short man and the chair was huge and high and faced away from the door, so that only red bristles which stuck up straight on top of the man's head could be seen.

The man in the chair said in a small, childlike voice, "Shoot off that gun, Habeas, or I'll tie knots in all your legs."

With an uncanny intelligence, the pig sat down, inserted a

hoof inside the trigger guard, and the gun went off with an ear-splitting report.

"Swell!" said the man in the chair. "Only you better stand, Habeas. Next time, the gun might be pointed at your posterior and there might not be a blank in it."

Doc Savage said, "Monk."

"Uh-huh," said the man in the chair. "Sure, Doc, what is it?"

"Willard Spanner was a friend of mine."

"MONK"—Lieutenant Colonel Andrew Blodgett Mayfair—lifted out of the chair. He was not much over five feet tall. He was only slightly less broad than that, and he had a pair of arms which gave the grotesque impression of being nearly as long as he was tall. Red hairs, which looked coarse as match sticks, furred his leathery hide. His was the build of a gorilla.

"I read about it in them blasted newspapers," he said, and his small voice was doubly ridiculous, contrasted with his physique. "Willard Spanner was seized in Frisco at noon. He was found dead here in New York at ten minutes to three. Screw loose somewhere."

Monk wrinkled a fabulously homely face to show puzzlement. He looked amiable, stupid, when, in truth, he was one of the most clever industrial chemists alive.

"Maybe the newspapers got balled up on the difference in time between San Francisco and New York," he added.

"All times given are New York time," Doc Savage said.

"Then the guy seized in San Francisco wasn't Willard Spanner, or the one dead here in New York isn't Spanner," Monk declared. "The bird didn't go from Frisco to New York in a little over two hours. It just isn't being done yet."

Doc Savage asked, "Any messages?"

"Ham phoned, and said he was coming up," replied the homely chemist. "I haven't been here long. Dunno what was recorded before I got here."

The bronze man went into the next room, which was a scientific laboratory, one of the most complete in existence, and crossed that to the vast, white-enameled room which held his laboratory of chemical, electrical and other devices. He lifted the cover on the telephone recorder robot, switched a loud-speaker and amplifier into circuit with the playback pickup, and started the mechanism.

Monk came in and listened, slackjawed, as the device reproduced the call from San Francisco, complete to its violent termination. The pig, Habeas—Habeas Corpus was the shote's full appendage—trailed at the homely chemist's heels.

Doc Savage examined the time stamped on the recording roll.

"Two minutes past twelve," he said.

"Was that Willard Spanner's voice, or would you know it?" Monk demanded.

"I would know his voice," Doc replied. "And that was, unquestionably, Willard Spanner."

"Speaking from San Francisco?" Monk grunted incredulously.

"We will see." Doc Savage made a call, checking with the telephone people, then hung up and advised, "The call came from San Francisco, all right. Willard Spanner appears to have been seized while he was in the booth making the call."

Monk picked the pig, Habeas, up by one oversize ear—a treatment the shote seemed not to mind.

"Then the dead man here in New York is not Willard Spanner," declared the simian chemist. "Nobody goes from Frisco to New York in not much more than two hours."

"We will see about that," Doc told him.

"How?"

"By visiting the New York morgue where the dead man was taken."

Monk nodded. "How about Ham?"

"We will leave him a note," Doc said.

APPARENTLY, it had not occurred to any one in authority on the New York civic scene that the surroundings of the dead were of æsthetic value, for the morgue building was a structure which nearly attained the ultimate in shoddiness.

Its brick walls gave the appearance of having not been washed in generations, being almost black with soot and city grime. The steps were grooved deep by treading feet, and the stone paving of the entry into which the dead wagons ran was rutted by tires. Rusting iron bars, very heavy, were over the windows; for just what reason, no one probably could have told.

"This joint gives me the creeps—and I don't creep easy," Monk imparted, as they got out of Doc Savage's roadster before the morgue.

The roadster was deceptively long. Its color was somber. The fact that its body was of armor plate, its windows —specially built in the roadster doors—of bullet-proof glass, was not readily apparent.

Monk carried Habeas Corpus by an ear and grumbled, "I wonder why anybody should kill Willard Spanner? Or grab him, either? Spanner was an all-right guy. He didn't have any enemies."

Doc listened at the entrance. There was silence, and no attendant was behind the reception desk where one should have been. They stepped inside.

"Hello, somebody!" Monk called.

Silence answered.

There was an odor in the air, a rather peculiar tang. Monk sniffed.

"Say, I knew they used formaldehyde around these places," he muttered. "But there's something besides——"

Doc Savage moved with such suddenness that he seemed to explode. But it was a silent explosion, and he was little more than a noiseless bronze blur as he crossed to the nearest door. He did not try to pass through the door, but flattened beside it.

Monk, bewildered, began, "Say, what the blazes? First I smell——"

A man came through the door, holding a big single-action six-gun. He said, "Start your settin'-up exercises, boys!" Then his eyes bulged, for he had apparently expected to see two men—and Doc Savage, beside the door, escaped his notice.

The man with the six-shooter was bony and looked as if he had been under bright suns much of his life. He wore a new suit, but his shirt was a coarse blue work garment, faded from washing. The tie was blue and looked as if it had been put on and taken off many times, without untying the knot. The knot was a very long one.

Doc Savage struck silently and with blinding speed. The gun wielder saw him, but could not move in time, and the bronze man's fist took him on the temple. The six-gun evidently had a hair trigger. It went off. The bullet made a hole, round and neat, in the wall behind Monk.

Monk began howling and charged for the door.

"Now ain't this somethin'!" he bellowed.

Doc Savage had gone on with a continuation of the dive which he had made at the six-gun wielder, and was already through the door. The room beyond was an office with four desks and four swivel chairs.

Five persons were arrayed on the floor. The morgue attendants, obviously. They were neither bound nor gagged, but they lay very still. The odor of chloroform was heavy in the air.

Two men were on their feet. One was tall, the other short, and the short one wore overall pants and his legs were bowed. Both were weather-beaten.

The tall one held in one hand a blue revolver and in the other a bandanna handkerchief, which gave off chloroform stench. The short man had an automatic rifle from which barrel and stock had been bobbed off short.

A bundle of clothing lay in the middle of the floor.

The automatic rifle smacked loudly as Doc came through the door. But the marksman did not lead his target quite enough. He shot again. The cartridge stuck in the ejector.

"Damn it!" the rifleman bawled.

"Throw it away!" gritted the tall man. "I told you that gun wouldn't work if you bobtailed it!"

The tall man danced back as he spoke, seeming in no hurry to shoot. He waved his blue revolver, that Doc Savage might be sure to see it.

"Don't be a sucker!" the man suggested. "Behave yourself."

Doc Savage held his hands out even with his shoulders and came to a stop, but not until momentum had carried him to the center of the room.

Monk lumbered through the door. He stopped, looked closely at the blue gun as if it were some strange animal, then put up his stub-fingered hands.

"That's bein' sensible," said the tall man. "I can bust poker chips in the air with this here hogleg. Stunted, there, is a good shot, too, only he thought he knew more about that auto rifle than the gent who made her."

"Stunted," the short man, was peering into the innards of his doctored rifle.

"Aw-w," he mumbled. "I took too much tension off the spring."

Monk grunted, "What's the idea, you guys?"

"We like to look at dead people," the tall man said dryly. "We're strange that way."

Doc Savage was standing with his toes almost against the bundle of clothing. The bundle was snug, being strapped around tightly with a belt.

Doc hooked a toe under the bundle and kicked with great force.

THE human nervous system is capable of registering

impressions only so fast. The tall man undoubtedly knew the missile was coming, but could do nothing. When it hit him, he recoiled instinctively.

The next instant, he was flat on his face, held there by one foot which Doc Savage jammed down on his neck.

Monk whooped loudly, rushed Stunted. Monk's fights were always noisy.

Stunted clung like a zealot to his bobtailed auto rifle, trying to get it in operation. He failed. He tried to club with the gun. Monk jerked it out of his hands as if he were taking a lollypop from a child, then dropped it.

Monk picked the short man up bodily, turned him over and dropped him on his head. He accomplished the motion with such speed that the short man was helpless. Stunted did not move after he fell on his head.

Monk blinked small eyes at his victim.

"Gosh," he said. "I wonder if that hurt him?"

The tall man on the floor snarled, "What in blue blazes kind of a circus is this, anyhow?"

Monk felt of Stunted's head, found it intact, then twisted one of the short man's rather oversize ears, but got no response. The homely chemist turned on the tall man.

"So it's a circus, huh?" he grunted. "I wondered."

"Aw, hell!" gritted the other.

Monk came over and sat on the lean prisoner. Doc Savage removed his foot from the man's neck. Monk grabbed the fellow's ears and pulled them. He seemed fascinated by the rubbery manner in which they stretched out from the man's head.

"They'd make swell souvenirs," Monk grunted.

"Cut it out!" the tall man howled. "What're you gonna do with me?"

"I'm gonna ask you questions," Monk told him. "And I'm gonna be awful mad if you don't answer 'em."

"Nuts!" said the captive.

"Has this raid, or whatever it was, got anything to do with Willard Spanner?" Monk asked.

"What do you think?" the other snapped.

Monk pulled the ears. Tears came to the man's eyes. He cursed, and his voice was a shrill whine of agony.

"I'll kill you for that!" he promised. "Damn me, if I don't!"

Monk shuddered elaborately, grinned and said, "If I had on boots, I'd shake in 'em. What did you come here for?"

A new voice said, "You gentlemen seem to be humorists."

MONK started violently and twisted his head toward the door. He gulped, "Blazes!" and got hastily to his feet.

The man in the door was solid, athletic-looking, and he held a revolver with familiar ease. He was in his socks. That probably explained how he had come in from the outside so silently: that, and the faint mumble of city traffic, which was always present.

"Get up!" he told the tall man. "Wipe your eyes. Then grab that bunch of clothes. This is sure something to write home about!"

"I'll kill this ape!" bawled the tall man.

"Some other time," the rescuer suggested. "Get the clothes. Say, just who is this big bronze guy and the monkey, anyhow?"

"How would I know?" snarled the man whom Monk had been badgering. He picked up the bundle of clothing and started for the door.

"You wouldn't leave Stunted, would you?" asked the first.

Without a word, the tall man picked up the short fellow and made his way, not without difficulty, out through the door.

The gun wielder looked on benignly. He had one stark peculiarity. His eyes were blue. And something was wrong with them. They crossed at intervals, pupils turning in toward the nose. Then they straightened out. The owner seemed to do the straightening with visible effort.

Monk demanded, "Who did them clothes belong to?"

The man said, "They'll answer a lot of questions where you're going."

Monk did not get a clear impression of what happened next. Things moved too fast. Doc Savage must have read the intention of the man with the queer eyes. Doc lunged.

The gun went off. But the man with the eyes had tried to shift from Monk to Doc for a target and had not quite made it. His bullet pocked the wall. Then Doc had a grip on the revolver.

The man let go of the revolver. He bounced back, fast on his feet, reached the door and sloped through. He was yelling now. His yells caused noise of other feet in the next room. There were evidently more men.

Doc grasped Monk and propelled him backward. They got into a rear room and slammed the door. Doc shot the bolt.

Revolver bullets chopped around the lock. Wood splintered. The lock held. A man kicked the door. Monk roared a threat.

There was no more kicking, no more shooting. Silence fell, except for the traffic noises.

Monk looked at Doc.

"That guy with the performing eyes was gonna kill us both," he mumbled.

Doc Savage did not comment. He listened, then unlocked the door. The room beyond was empty. He advanced. In the next room, one of the chloroformed morgue attendants was sitting up and acting sick.

The street outside held no sign of the violent raiders. There was no trace of the bundle of clothing.

The reviving morgue attendant began to mumble.

"They wanted clothes off a corpse," he muttered. "Whatcha know about that?"

"Off what corpse?" Doc asked him.

"Off Willard Spanner," said the attendant.

Chapter 2

THE HIGH-PRESSURE GHOULS

DOC SAVAGE exited to the street and made inquiries, finding that the men had gone away in two cars. Persons questioned named four different makes of cars, in each instance insisting that their information was correct.

"They're all wrong, probably," Monk grumbled.

Pursuit was patently hopeless, although Monk cast a number of expectant glances in Doc Savage's direction. The bronze man had a way of pulling rabbits out of hats in affairs such as this. But Doc only reëntered the morgue. None of those who had been chloroformed were in immediate danger.

"We came here to see the body of Willard Spanner," Doc told the attendant who had revived.

"Sort of a coincidence," said the attendant, and managed a sickly grin which typified a peculiarity of human behavior—the fact that persons who work regularly in close proximity to death are inclined to arm themselves with a wise-cracking veneer.

The bodies were stored in bins not unlike huge filing boxes. The marble slabs on which they lay slid into the bins on rollers. The attendant was still too groggy to bring the Willard Spanner slide out after he had found the identifying card, and Monk helped him.

Doc Savage looked at the body for a long time.

"This is Willard Spanner," he said finally."

They went out.

Monk scratched his head, then said, "But the man seized in San Francisco—that couldn't have been Willard Spanner."

"The voice on the phone recorder," Doc reminded.

"You said it was Willard Spanner's voice." Monk found his pig, Habeas, and picked him up by an ear. "Could you have been mistaken about that voice?"

"I think not," Doc Savage said slowly.

They examined those who were still senseless from the chloroform, gave a description of the morgue raiders to police officers who had arrived, then walked out to the roadster.

Monk seemed to be thinking deeply. He snapped his fingers.

"That bundle of Willard Spanner's clothing!" he grumbled. "Now what in the dickens did they want with that? The police had searched the pockets and had found nothing."

"It must have been something important," Doc told him. "They wanted the garments badly enough to make quite a disturbance in getting them."

A policeman came to the morgue door and called, "You are wanted on the phone."

Doc and Monk went back, and Doc picked up the receiver and said, "Yes?" inquiringly.

A clipped, melodious voice spoke rapidly. It was the voice of an orator, and it carried the accent which is commonly associated with Harvard.

"I got to the morgue in time to observe that something was badly wrong," advised the speaker. "I followed the chaps outside when they left in such a hurry. They are now at Albemarle Avenue and Frame Street. I will meet you at the corner."

Doc Savage said, "In ten minutes," and hung up.

Monk, making for the street in a series of ungainly bounds, demanded, "Who was it?"

"Ham," Doc replied.

"The shyster!" Monk growled, and there was infinite contempt in his tone.

ALBEMARLE AVENUE was a twin groove through marsh mud on the outskirts of New York City. Frame Street seemed to be a sign, scabby and ancient, which stuck out of the salt grass. If there ever had been a Frame Street, it had long ago given up to the swamp.

Darkness was coming on when Doc Savage and Monk arrived in the roadster.

"There's Ham," Monk said.

"Ham" was Brigadier General Theodore Marley Brooks, Park Avenue fashion plate, and a lawyer, the pride of Harvard law school. He was a slender man with the manner of a wasp and a tongue as sharp as the fine Damascus sword blade concealed in the innocent-looking black cane which he carried.

He came out of the marsh grass, stepping gingerly to avoid soiling his natty afternoon garb, the sword cane tucked under an arm.

"Hy-ah, you fashion plate," Monk growled.

"Hello, stupid," Ham retorted insultingly.

The two glared at each other. A stranger would have thought fisticuffs imminent. As a matter of fact, each of these two had time and again risked his life to save the other, although no one had ever heard one of them address a civil word to the other.

Ham opened the roadster door on Doc Savage's side, and said, "I got the note you left at headquarters, telling me you had gone to the morgue. I went to the morgue. As I said over the phone—those chaps were clowning around, so I followed them."

"Where are they?" Doc asked.

Ham pointed across the swamp. "An oyster plant over there."

"Oyster plant?" Monk grunted.

"They probably use it as a blind for whatever they are doing," Ham offered. "And, incidentally, just what is behind this?"

"It's all screwy, so far," Monk snorted. "Willard Spanner is reported grabbed in Frisco at noon, and is found dead in New York before three o'clock. Then a gang of birds raid the morgue and steal his clothing. That's all we know."

Ham said, "I'll show you where they went. They had that bundle of clothing, too."

There were a few comparatively firm spots in the marsh. The rest of the terrain was covered with water which ranged in depth from an inch to two feet, with spots which were deeper, as Monk promptly proved by going in above the waist.

A cloud bank in the west shortened the period of twilight. They were soon in complete darkness. Using flashlights would have given away their position. Making any speed through the coarse grass, without noise, was almost impossible.

"You fellows take it easy," Doc directed. "Do not try to get too close."

Monk began, "But what're you——" and did not finish. The bronze man had vanished in the darkness.

Monk listened, then shook his head. It was difficult to conceive of any one moving with such silence.

It was no casual trait, this ability of Doc Savage's to stalk quietly. He had practiced a great deal, had studied the masters of the art: the carnivorous beasts of the jungle.

The bronze man had covered not more than a hundred yards when something happened—something that was, later, to take on great significance and a terrible importance.

He heard a peculiar crashing sound. That described it more accurately than anything else. It was not a series of crashes, but one long, brittle report. It started faintly and attained, in the span of two seconds or so, a surprising loudness.

Doc glanced up. Hanging in the sky was what appeared to be a taut rope of liquid fire. This faded in a moment.

It was an uncanny phenomena.

Doc Savage crouched for some time, listening, flake-gold eyes on the sky. But there was nothing more. He went on toward the oyster plant.

The odor of the place was evident long before the low, rambling processing building showed up. It was built on the beach, with a wharf shoving out porch fashion to one side. A channel had evidently been dredged for the oyster boats. The plant was used for the sorting and opening of oysters.

Mounds of oyster shells were pyramided here and there, and were thick on the ground. They made walking difficult. Wash of waves on the near-by beach covered up lesser sounds.

Several times Doc Savage stooped and brushed away oyster shells, that he might step on the bare ground. The brittle shells would break with loud reports. The side of the building which he approached was dark. He worked around. Lighted windows appeared.

Smell of oysters was strong. Two small schooners were tied up at a wharf. The cabin portholes of one of these were lighted. An instant later, the light went out, and three men came up the companion. They stepped to the wharf. One used a flashlight, and this illuminated them.

One was Stunted. His companions were the tall man and the one with the peculiar crossing and uncrossing eyes. One carried a bundle which resembled clothing.

Stunted said, "Danged if I don't still maintain that an automatic rifle can be bobbed and still———"

"Aw, hell!" The tall man spat disgustedly. "Here we really got things to worry about, and you go on and on about that gun. Man, don't the fact that that bronze guy was Doc Savage impress you none a-tall?"

Stunted stopped suddenly.

"Look, you gents," he said. "You been cackling around like two old hens since you learned that bird was Doc Savage. Now I want you to tell me something."

"Yeah?" said the tall man.

"Ain't it a fact that with what we got, we don't need to be afraid of anybody?" demanded Stunted.

"You mean———"

"You know what I mean. You saw that streak in the sky and heard that crack of a noise, a while ago, didn't you? Now answer my question."

"Aw-w-w!" The tall man spat again. "We ain't exactly afraid of him. Only it might've been more convenient if he hadn't turned up on the spot. That Savage is nobody's cinch, and don't forget that."

"I ain't forgettin' it," said Stunted. "And quit squawkin', you hombres. We're settin' pretty. Doc Savage ain't got a line on us. And didn't we get Willard Spanner's clothing. And ain't the rest gonna be taken care of?"

The tall man burst into sudden laughter.

"Now what?" Stunted growled.

"Just thinkin'," the other chuckled. "People are gonna wonder how Willard Spanner was in Frisco at noon and dead here in New York at three o'clock the same afternoon."

DOC SAVAGE was close to them. He could have reached out and tripped any one of the trio as they filed past.

The silent man of the three, the one with the unnaturally roving eyes, brought up the rear. Doc Savage had been crouching. He stood erect. His fist made a sound like a loud finger snap on the man's jaw. The man fell. The bundle of clothing flew to one side.

A number of surprising things happened. The surrounding

darkness erupted human beings. At least a dozen men appeared with magical effect. Each had a flashlight, a gun.

"Take 'im alive?" one shouted questioningly.

"Not much!" squawled another, evidently the chief.

Doc started for the clothing bundle. A man was leaping over it, coming toward him, gun spouting flame and thunder. Doc sloped aside. He twisted. Lead slammed past.

Doc hit the ground and rolled. Tall marsh grass took him in. He burrowed a dozen feet, veered left. Slugs tore through the grass. They made hoarse snarls.

A pile of oyster shells jutted out of the darkness in front of him. The bronze man got behind it. He ran a score of paces, went down in a hollow where there was soft mud, but no water, and waited, listening.

Stunted was yelling, "He's behind that shell pile! If I had an auto rifle, it would put a pill right through that stuff!"

"Suppose you use your legs more and your mouth less!" some one suggested.

The men scattered, hunting. They were in pairs, a neat precaution. The couples did not walk close enough together that both could be surprised at once, yet nothing could happen to one without the other knowing it.

Stunted shouted, "You jaspers knew he was around here! How in thunder did you know that?"

"You wouldn't understand," a voice told him.

Stunted swore at the speaker. "C'mon, feller, how'd you know it?"

"There's a bank of alarm wires strung around here," said the voice.

"Nuts!" Stunted told him. "I haven't seen any wires."

"They're underground," the other snapped. "Just barely covered. Any one walking over them changes the capacity of a high-frequency electric field enough to show on a recording device inside."

"Well, sink me!" Stunted snorted.

Doc Savage, listening, made a mental note that some one of considerable scientific ability was involved with the gang. Such an alarm system as had been described was feasible, but required high technical knowledge to construct.

The bronze man crawled away through the tall grass.

Doc did not go far, however. A score of yards, and he stopped. He spent a moment or two tensing his throat muscles, striving for a certain effect.

"Hands up, you fellows!" he said loudly, using his own natural voice.

A split of a second later, he shouted again. This time, his tone was a splendid imitation of a man greatly frightened.

"It's Doc Savage!" he shrilled. "Give us a hand over here, somebody!"

Results were instant and noisy. Men howled irately and made a great clatter in the marsh grass, charging for the spot. They were completely deceived.

Doc Savage moved swiftly, not in flight but circling back toward the oyster shell mound near which he had made his attack. He wanted the bundle of clothes.

He reached the shell pile, paused, listened. Men were making angry sounds, but not close by. Some one had dropped a flashlight in the excitement. Its beam did not play directly on the spot where the garments lay, but the backglow disclosed the parcel. It was hardly more than thirty feet away. It lay in the open.

Doc continued listening. His ears were remarkable, for he had trained them from childhood with a sonic device calculated to develop the utmost in sensitivity. He evidently caught some small sound, for he produced from inside his clothing a coil of thin silken cord to which was affixed a folding grapple hook.

That he had practiced a great deal with the grapple was shown by the accuracy with which he tossed the hook. It snared the bundle of clothing. He hauled it toward him, remaining sheltered behind the shell pile.

Stunted and other men bounded up from where they had been lying and watching the bundle.

"He slicked us!" Stunted bawled.

Doc Savage gave the silk cord a brisk yank, stooped, and caught the garments, and was off like a sprinter. Guns made whooping thunder behind him. He pitched right, then left, zigzagging. Then he doubled over and changed course.

The last was a wise move. Some type of light machine gun blared out behind him. Its lead stream sickled off the marsh grass across the spot where he had vacated. The gunman did not fan his fire, but concentrated it, and the ammo drum went empty. Violent cursing followed.

Doc was some distance away now. He heard noises of men sloughing about in mud, and enraged grunts and growls.

"Monk!" he called softly. "Ham!"

The pair were waist-deep in mud. Doc extricated them. They joined him in flight.

"Monk, the baboon, led us into that bog!" Ham complained.

Monk found his pet pig before he shouted, "That's a lie! I was followin' that overdressed shyster!"

Sounds of pursuit dropped rapidly behind, and it became evident that they were going to get clear.

"We oughta do something about them rambunctious jaspers," Monk announced.

"The police will do something about it," Doc told him.

DOC SAVAGE, Monk, and Ham were in the skyscraper headquarters when the police telephoned the results of their raid, staged on the strength of the bronze man's information.

The oyster factory, they advised, had been found deserted. The "birds" had flown.

"They must have a bally tight organization to move that fast," Ham opined. "They knew their hangout was no longer a secret, so they cleared out."

Monk lifted his pig, Habeas, by one oversize ear and swayed the porker slowly back and forth, a procedure the shote seemed to enjoy.

"What gets me," muttered the homely chemist, "is what that streak of a thing in the sky could have been. Did you see it, Doc?"

The bronze man nodded.

Monk persisted, "Hear the funny long crack of a noise it, or something like it, made?"

Doc nodded again, then said, "The men at the oyster factory mentioned the streak in the sky and the sound, as having some mysterious connection with their own project."

Monk let Habeas fall. "Say, what's behind all of this, anyway?"

The telephone rang.

"This is the central police station," a voice stated. "You seemed to be interested in that Willard Spanner killing, so I thought we'd better let you know his body has been stolen from the morgue."

"You mean Willard Spanner's clothing was stolen?" Doc queried.

"I mean his body," said the officer. "They got his clothing first. They came back about fifteen minutes ago for the body."

"Same crowd?"

"Sure."

"They got away?"

"They did. Or they have, so far."

Doc had switched an audio amplifier-and-loud-speaker into

circuit with the telephone, a procedure he commonly followed on calls in which his aides might be interested. Monk
and Ham heard.

"Jove!" Ham exploded. "They made no move to take the
body the first time."

"At the oyster factory, I heard them speaking of 'taking
care of the rest,'" Doc said slowly. "This matter of the body
must have been the 'rest.'"

Ham lifted the bundle of clothing which Doc Savage had
taken at the oyster factory.

"We still have Willard Spanner's garments here," he declared. "Since those men wanted them so badly, they may
possibly furnish us with a clue."

Monk got up, grunting, "Maybe the duds had papers or
something sewed in them, like they have in story books. Let's
have a gander at 'em, as we lowbrows say."

The garments were tied together with tarred twine of the
type which seagoing men call marlin. Ham took hold of it,
after trying the knot, intending to break it; but finding it
much stronger than he had expected, gave it up, grimacing,
snapping his strained fingers.

Doc examined the knots.

"No sailor tied those," he decided.

"They didn't talk like sailors, either," Monk offered. "What
part of the country d'you figure they came from, Doc?"

"The West, or the Southwest," the bronze man said, and,
with no perceptible difficulty, broke the cord which had
baffled Ham. He sorted through the pieces of clothing.

"They outfoxed us," he said. "Fixed this up as a decoy by
that shell pile merely to draw me back, hoping to get a shot
at me."

Monk squinted. "Meaning?"

"These are not Willard Spanner's clothes," Doc said.
"They are for a much larger and fatter man."

Monk groaned, "We're sunk!"

"We have," Doc corrected him, "one chance."

Chapter 3

THE MAN FROM OKLAHOMA

THE bronze man lifted the telephone receiver and dialed a number.

"Police headquarters?" he asked. . . . "Homicide bureau, please." There was a brief wait. "Homicide? . . . This is Doc Savage speaking. I believe it is your custom to secure pictures of murder scenes, and also photographs of the body of the victim. I wonder if you would send me copies of the pictures taken of Willard Spanner."

"You can have them," advised the voice at the homicide bureau.

"By messenger, immediately," Doc requested.

That he had been promised the photographs so readily was not remarkable, since the bronze man held a high commission, no whit less effective because it was honorary, on the New York police force. The commission was a gesture of appreciation for past aid.

Doc Savage's life work was helping others out of trouble—those who deserved aid. It was a strange career, one with few financial rewards. But the bronze man did not need money, for he had access to a fabulous treasure trove. He followed his career for the return it gave in excitement and adventure. And he had five aides who followed it for the same reason.

Monk and Ham were two of the five. The other three were, at the moment, in upper New York State, where Doc Savage maintained a remarkable institution for making honest men out of such criminals as he caught, a treatment which entailed brain operations and which wiped out past memories. A course of vocational training followed the surgery.

Monk frowned, demanding, "How in the heck are those pictures gonna help us?"

Doc Savage did not answer, seemed not to hear. Monk showed no resentment at not getting an answer. It happened

frequently. The homely chemist went out and came back
with late editions of the leading newspapers.

"Lookit!" He pointed at headlines.

UNPREDICTED RAIN OF COMETS
SCIENCE CANNOT EXPLAIN

Those residents of New York City, particularly those
residing near the marsh section of Long Island, were treated
to the sight of a comet to-night. Many reported a loud crack
of a sound and a streak of fire in the sky.

Inquiry develops that such phenomena have been reported
within the last few days, from various sections of the United
States.

Monk said, "And they kindly neglected to state just where
the other comets were seen."

"Telephone the newspapers," Doc requested.

Monk went to the instrument, made several calls, and hung
up, wearing a puzzled expression.

"The comets have appeared within the last two weeks," he
reported. "Several were seen around San Francisco. That
kinda hooks in with this Willard Spanner killing. But most of
the comets were seen in Oklahoma, around Tulsa."

Doc Savage was examining the bundle of clothing.

"Come here," he said, and pointed at the label inside the
coat.

THE OIL MAN'S TAILOR
TULSA, OKLAHOMA.

Monk grunted, "That'll bear looking into."

Doc Savage put in a long-distance telephone call, and because it was late, some time was required in obtaining the information which he desired. In the interim, a messenger arrived from police headquarters with a parcel of pictures. Finally, the bronze man secured from the Tulsa tailor, the
name of the man for whom a suit answering the description
of the one in the bundle had been made. It was a suit distinctive enough to be remembered, being rather loud in color.

"The garment was tailored for Calvert R. Moore, who is
more commonly known as 'Leases' Moore," came the report
from Tulsa.

"Just what do you know about this man Moore?" Doc
asked.

"He is very wealthy." The Tulsa tailor hesitated. "He is

also considered a bit sharp as a business man. Nothing crooked, you understand. Merely, well—a man who misses few bargains."

"What else?"

"He has disappeared?"

"He has what?"

"Disappeared."

"A kidnaping?" Doc demanded.

"There has been no indication of that. Leases Moore merely dropped out of sight two weeks ago, on the same day that Quince Randweil vanished."

"Quince Randweil?" Doc asked sharply. "Who is he?"

"The owner and operator of a local dog-racing track," explained the tailor.

"There is no indication of what became of these men?" Doc persisted.

"None."

"Have either of these men been considered crooked?" Doc asked.

"Oh, they ain't neither one been in jail, that anybody knows of," said the tailor, who seemed to be a frank and talkative individual.

Monk squinted at Doc when the conversation ended. "More angles?"

"Two men named Leases Moore and Quince Randweil vanished mysteriously in Tulsa, two weeks ago," Doc told him. "Leases Moore's clothing turned up in that bundle."

The bronze man now scrutinized the pictures of Willard Spanner's body. Spanner had been shot to death. Two bullets had hit him in the chest.

But it was another wound a wrist cut, upon which the bronze man concentrated attention.

"This was not a new cut," he pointed out. "You will notice marks made by adhesive tape, indicating it was bandaged. The manner of the tape application indicates the work of a physician. The man would hardy have applied the tape himself in this manner. I observed this fact at the morgue, but unfortunately, not close enough to be sure."

Monk looked surprised. It was not often that the bronze man had to go back over ground he had already covered for information.

"But where's this getting us?" asked the homely chemist.

"Our problem is to ascertain whether the man seized in

San Francisco was the one found dead in New York," Doc told him. "On the face of it, that seems an impossibility—for less than three hours elapsed."

Doc resorted to the long-distance telephone again. He first called San Francisco police. They gave him the name of the hotel at which Willard Spanner had been staying. Incidental was the information that Spanner had arrived in San Francisco only the previous day.

The call to the hotel was fruitful. Willard Spanner had slipped in the hotel bathroom, struck his arm against a glass shelf over the washstand, and the shelf had broken, cutting his wrist. The hotel physician had dressed the wound, which was undoubtedly the one the pictures showed.

"Whew!" Monk exploded. "Willard Spanner *was* seized in San Francisco a little over a couple o' hours before he was found dead in New York!"

Ham flourished his sword cane. "But it could not happen!"

Monk stood up. "The telephoning has taken time. There oughta be fresh newspapers out. I'll go get some."

He was back in a few moments. He looked excited.

"Lamp this!" he barked, and exhibited extra editions.

The headlines were large, black.

SEEK SPANNER RANSOM IN FRISCO—$50,000 DEMANDED

A San Francisco newspaper editor late to-day received a note stating that Willard Spanner, reported slain in New York this afternoon, was alive, and would be released upon the payment of fifty thousand dollars.

There was more of it, but the opening paragraph told the substance of the story.

Monk eyed Doc. "Hadn't we better look into this? Ham or me can go."

"We will all three go," Doc told him. "We will leave a note advising the other three members of our outfit to do what investigating they can, when they return from up-State. They can handle the New York end."

"What about the Tulsa, Oklahoma, angle?" Ham queried.

"We will stop off there," Doc advised.

TULSA likes to call itself the capital of the oil industry. Oil men do much flying. The Tulsa municipal airport is a source of local pride. Facilities and appointments are excellent.

Floodlights fanned brilliance as Doc Savage dropped his big speed plane in for a landing. The night force of mechanics stood about and stared. Some one ran to a near-by flying school, and shortly afterward there was a stampede to the tarmac of aëronautical students in all states of partial dress. It was not often that a plane such as the bronze man was flying was seen.

The speed ship was trimotored, and all three motors were streamlined into the wings until their presence was hardly apparent to the eye. The hull breasted down so that the plane could be landed on water, and the landing gear was retractable. The cabin was as bulletproof as was feasible, and inside were innumerable mechanical devices.

One individual did not seem interested in the bronze man's remarkable craft. He was a pilot in greasy coveralls who tinkered with the motor of a shabby-looking cabin monoplane over near the edge of the field.

He had dropped into the airport two hours before, and had been tinkering with his plane since. He had given short answers to the field mechanics, and thereafter had been left severely alone. It was now not long before dawn.

Doc Savage taxied over near the covered pit which held the gasoline hoses and cut all three motors. He stepped out of the plane and glanced into the east, as if seeking the sunrise.

"I've heard a lot about that bird," a flying student said, unconscious that his whisper carried. "They say he designed that sky wagon himself and that it's the fastest thing of its size in the world."

Over at the edge of the field, the motor of the shabby cabin monoplane came to life. It roared loudly.

A small crowd surged around Doc's speed ship. They were flying men, greatly interested in a sample of the most advanced aërial conveyance. Most of them were interested in the layout of navigating instruments, in the robot pilot.

"I've heard this bus can take off and fly herself, and can be controlled by radio from a distance," a man said. "Is that a fact?"

One man was interested in the tail structure of the plane. He found himself alone back there. He flashed a long knife out of his clothing, ripped and gouged, and got open one of the inspection ports through which the control connections could be examined.

The man was thin; his movements had the speed of an animal. He whipped a series of three packages out of his clothing. They were connected by wires, and none were extraordinarily large. He thrust all three inside the inspection port, then closed the flap. Then he backed away into the darkness.

He blinked a small flashlight four times rapidly.

Motor a-howl, the cabin monoplane scudded away from the edge of the field. It headed straight for Doc's ship.

THE bronze man had to all appearances been occupied entirely in answering questions. But now he flashed into life, and seemed to know exactly what he was doing.

"Run!" he rapped at those standing about. "Get away from here! Quick!"

His great voice was a crash. It was compelling. Three men turned and fled without knowing why. The others retreated more slowly. They saw the oncoming cabin plane.

"Runaway ship!" some one howled.

Monk and Ham had stepped out of Doc's speed craft. They whirled to clamber back inside. But Doc Savage was ahead of them. He banged the cabin door in their faces, then lunged to the controls. The big motors whooped out at the first touch of the starters, and because they were hot, instantly hauled the speed craft ino motion.

There was a tense second or two. Then it became evident that Doc's plane was going to get clear. The men scattered from the path of the oncoming cabin monoplane. It went bawling past, doing no harm, except to give an aviator student a bad fright.

All who looked could see by the floodlight glare that the cabin was empty.

"Where's the pilot of that trap?" yelled the night field manager. "Such damned carelessness——"

He swallowed the rest. An unexpected thing was happening. A weird thing.

The old cabin ship had gone on, but instead of crashing into the fence at the edge of the field, as every one expected, it was turning—swinging as if a hand of uncanny skill were at the controls. It arched completely around and cannoned after the speed plane of Doc Savage.

The onlookers gasped, unable to believe what they were witnessing. They saw the pig, Habeas Corpus, come hurtling from the cabin of Doc's speed ship. Then they saw the bronze man appear in the cabin door.

He seemed to be trying to reach the tail of his plane, for he dropped off and sought to seize it as it went past. But the streamlined metal surface offered no grip. He was knocked aside and the ship went on.

Doc scrambled to all fours, seized the pig, Habeas, and fell flat with him. He lay there.

The shabby cabin ship charged in pursuit of the speed plane. The two ships approached at an angle. They met. The whole world seemed to go up in blinding white.

The tarmac jumped, quaked. Windows fell out of operations office, hangars, the flying school buildings across the paved road. The side of one huge hangar buckled inward, and the roof came down as if a giant had stepped upon it.

The noise of the blast thumped and rolled and finally went into the distance like a heavy salvo of thunder.

Out where the two planes had met, there was a hole in the earth which would require two days to fill.

Chapter 4

OKLAHOMA ACTION

DOC SAVAGE heaved up from where he had lain after failing to reach the tail of his plane. He ran—not toward the blast scene, but toward his men. Monk and Ham veered out to meet him, Ham unconsciously knocking dust off his natty raiment.

"Why'd you quit the plane?" Monk gulped. "Why didn't you take it into the air?"

"We were low on gas," Doc clipped. "That other ship probably had full tanks. It would have caught me. Come on!"

"But there wasn't nobody in it!" Monk exploded as he ran.

"Radio control," Doc told him, racing toward the edge of the flying field. "The ship was loaded with explosive!"

Monk and Ham pounded in his wake. The pig, Habeas, trailed.

Monk puffed, "But no radio control would——"

"This was a device which would send the plane toward a sending set operating on a designated frequency," Doc advised over his shoulder. "It is merely an adaption of the robot pilot which keeps planes in the path of a beam radio."

Monk yelled, "But there wasn't no sending set in our bus!" He ran with the waddling gait of a scared bull ape.

"On the contrary, there was," Doc rapped. "A fellow stuck

a tiny portable set inside the empennage shortly before the excitement started. I saw him. There wasn't time to grab him."

"Where'd he go?" Monk roared, and put on more speed.

"This way," Doc said, and vaulted the metal fence which surrounded the field.

Ham tried to use too much care in mounting the fence, with the result that he slipped, caught his immaculate afternoon coat on the barbed top strand and left the entire back of it behind.

"Where'd the pilot of the plane go?" he gritted.

"This way," Doc said. "He and the fellow who planted the decoy radio transmitter probably intended to meet."

They covered a hundred yards. Weeds about them were tall. The rotating beacon at the airport flashed white light at regular intervals. The airport floodlights were still on, making a great glow.

Doc Savage stopped, breathed a "Listen!"

Monk and Ham both strained their ears. They heard crickets, sounds of distant automobiles and voice murmur back at the flying field, but nothing else.

"The two are heading a bit to the right," Doc decided.

Monk and Ham showed no surprise, being aware of the bronze man's almost superhuman ability to hear. Countless times, they had seen him employ the sonic device with which he had developed his aural organs over a period of years.

Weeds became more profuse, then ended suddenly at the edge of an evidently little used road. There was a fence which they managed to keep from squeaking while climbing it. Clouds were making the night darker than before. They crawled up an embankment, evidently some kind of dike. Hulks like gigantic pill boxes loomed ahead. The night air acquired a definite odor.

"Oil tank farm," Ham decided in a whisper.

"Not being used," Doc added.

Ham asked in a surprised tone, "How can you tell?"

"The odor," Doc told him. "The smell of fresh crude oil is lacking."

Off to the side, a smaller, squarer hulk appeared. A light came on suddenly and whitened soiled windows. Inside was the gleam of dull gray machinery and brasswork which needed cleaning.

"The pump station," Monk grunted. "They must be using it for a headquarters."

Ham offered abruptly, "Doc, what say the missing link and

myself circle and watch the rear, while you are reconnoitering?"

"Do not get too close," Doc requested.

Ham eased away in the darkness, Monk on his heels. The pig, Habeas, trailed them. They made half a circle and were behind the pump station. There was a pile of pipe there. They eased behind that.

Two men arose from the darkness and put guns against their backs.

"What the——" Monk began.

"I know it's a shame," said one of the men. "You two boys must have thought we were pretty dumb."

MONK and Ham turned around. There was not much light, but they did not need light to observe that the guns were genuine, and of large caliber. The hammer of each weapon was also rocked back.

Habeas, the shote, faded away into the night with the soundlessness of a shadow.

Monk jutted his small head forward to peer more closely at the two who had sprung the surprise.

"You'll get eyestrain," one of the men admonished. "We're the two yahoos you followed here from the airport, if that's what's worryin' you."

The speech had been in whispers, unconsciously. Now Ham decided to speak aloud, hoping to advise Doc of their predicament.

"You two—*ugh!*"

He doubled over painfully. His mouth flew wide, and breath came past his teeth with such force that it carried a fine spray with it.

The man who had jammed a gun into Ham's middle with great force hissed, "We know the bronze guy is around in front. You try to tip him again and you'll spring a leak just about the third button of that trick vest!"

The other man said, "We hate to part you two from that big bronze shadow, but we fear we must. Shake a leg."

They backed away from the pump station, came to a path, and went down it. Monk and Ham were searched expertly as they walked, and relieved of the only weapons they carried—the small supermachine pistols which were Doc Savage's own invention.

"What's the idea?" Monk demanded.

"A gentleman wants to see you," one of the two replied.

"Who?"

"A man whom I'm more than half convinced is one of the cleverest gents in the world," said the other. "And mind you, partner, I know all about the rep of this Doc Savage."

"The guy who thought up that bright idea of fixing the plane bomb so it would chase a radio transmitter, and who also rigged up that burglar alarm at the oyster plant in New York?" Monk hazarded.

"Sure," said the man. "He's thought of some other things that would surprise you, too."

"Shut up!" advised the man's companion. "Some day you'll talk yourself inside a wooden jacket, and they'll sprinkle some nice clean dirt on you."

They went on in silence. There was roadway underfoot now—a dirt road, hard packed by heavy traffic.

"What about Doc?" Ham demanded.

"We ain't ambitious," said one of the captors. "We'll dispose of *you* first. He'll get his later."

They rounded a bend fringed by scrub oak and came suddenly upon a truck waiting. The truck was large and had a flat bed, the type of machine employed in hauling pipe and oilfield supplies.

A stubby man came forward, also a tall, thin one and a man who had, when flashlights were turned on, eyes which turned inward at intervals. It was Stunted and the rest of the coterie from New York.

"It's a regular reunion," Stunted chuckled.

"You got that sawed-off auto rifle to working?" Monk asked him.

"You bet," Stunted retorted. "I worked on it all the way from New York."

"You made a quick trip," Monk suggested.

"Sure," said Stunted. "We came in a——"

The man with the uneasy eyes whipped forward and slapped Stunted in the face. The force of the blow sent Stunted reeling back.

"What in blue blazes was the idea?" he snarled.

"You got a head like a toad," the man with the weird eyes snapped. "You was gettin' set to tell this monkey how we came back!"

"Huh!" Stunted fell silent, his mien sheepish.

Two pairs of greasy overalls and two equally soiled jumpers were produced. Menace of gun muzzles persuaded Monk and Ham to don these. They were compelled to sit on the flat bed of the truck, legs dangling over, and the machine got into motion.

Some of the captors stood erect on the bed platform. All wore work clothing. They might have been some pipeline crew, bound into the fields.

"Let out a bleat and we'll certainly weight you down with lead," Monk and Ham were advised.

"Deuced boorish treatment," Ham said primly.

Some one laughed. The truck had a rear and gear grind and the sound went on and on, like something in pain. There was little traffic on the road, passenger cars for the most part. Once two policemen on motorcycles went past with a violent popping, but did not even glance at the truck.

Later, a ramshackle delivery car ran around the truck with a great clatter, cut in sharply and went on.

"Durn nut!" growled the truck driver.

Hardly more than ten minutes later, there was a loud report from a front wheel. The truck began to pound along in a manner which indicated a flat tire. The driver pulled over to the edge of the road. He began to swear, making no effort to get out and start repairs.

"You waiting for it to thunder, or something?" Stunted demanded.

"No spare tire along," said the driver. He alighted and used a flashlight until he found a large-headed roofing nail embedded in the tire. He kicked the nail and swore some more.

Down the road, a light flashed.

"Who's that?" a man demanded.

One of the men advanced down the road, keeping in the darker shadows beside the ditch. He returned soon.

"Delivery truck with a puncture," he reported. "It's that nut who passed us. He must've picked up another of them nails."

"He got a spare tire?" Stunted demanded.

"Seems to have," said the other.

Stunted chuckled. "Old Nick takes care of his own, eh, boys?"

Two guns were kept jammed against Monk and Ham. Three men went forward. There was a wait, during which pounding noises came from the delivery truck, then a sharp exchange of commands. One of the men called back, "Come on, you birds."

The guns urged Monk and Ham forward. They came to the truck.

The driver was an unusual-looking fellow, having a tremendous girth and a right leg which twisted out in grotesque fashion. His face was puffy. He had a swarthy skin and dark hair.

"This Mexican has kindly consented to give us a lift," chuckled Stunted, and flourished his sawed-off auto rifle at the swarthy driver.

The driver wailed, "Señors, my poor car——"

"Shut up!" advised Stunted. "You just drive us carefullike. We'll tell you where to go."

An hour later, they were traveling where there seemed to be no road at all. The sun was rising, but not yet in view.

"Turn right," Stunted advised, and they pulled down a precipitous bank and took to the gravel bed of a dry stream.

The swarthy driver complained, "Señors, my poor car will never run back over thees road. Tell me, how shall I return?"

"You'll find out all about that," Stunted told him.

"Hey!" one of the men barked. "Lookit!"

They craned necks. After a moment of that, they all heard a long, rending crack of a sound, and a weird streak of luminance appeared in the reddening sky. It seemed to stretch in an arch away into the infinite reaches of the heavens.

"Now, what?" Stunted grumbled. "Could that mean that——"

"Shut up, stupid!" the man with the peculiar eyes rapped.

The streak in the sky had died away quickly, vanishing completely.

The rickety truck went on. In spite of the deserted appearance of the region, it was undoubtedly a road of sorts which they traveled. Twice, when they crossed sandy stretches, the men alighted and, with leafy boughs, carefully brushed out their tracks.

"Don't want 'em to look too recent," Stunted grinned.

The driver showed alarm. "What ees thees mean, señores?"

"In about three minutes, you'll know," Stunted leered.

The driver reacted in a fashion which was the more surprising, since he had previously shown a surprisingly small degree of backbone. He lashed out a fist toward Stunted.

It was a terrific blow. After it, Stunted's face would never look quite the same. Stunted fell out of the seat.

The driver emitted a blood-curdling yell and took to the opposite direction. He had chosen his spot well. A narrow rip of a draw entered the creek bed at that point. The dark man dived into that. His game leg seemed, if anything, to add to his speed. He disappeared.

The truck unloaded in roaring confusion. Wild shots were discharged. The men rushed into the gully. Some climbed the steep sides. After the first excitement, they used flashlights and searched more thoroughly. They found no trace of the fugitive.

"One of that guy's ancestors must have been a rabbit," Stunted grumbled.

They consulted for a time. There seemed to be little they could do about it.

"That Mex won't know what it's all about, anyhow," some one decided.

They got in the truck, and it had rolled hardly less than half a mile before it pulled out on a flat and stopped before what seemed to be literally a mansion.

It was a great brick building, two stories in height, with flanking wings and a garage capable of housing four cars. Situated on the outskirts of a city such as Tulsa, the mansion would have aroused no more than admiration, but located here in a wilderness of scrub oak and hills, with no roads worthy of the name near by, it was a startling sight.

The headlights played on the place at closer range, and it became evident in the early morning light that many of the windows were broken out, that the woodwork needed painting, that the lawn had not been trimmed in years. Yet the place could not, from the style of architecture, have been more than ten years old.

Monk asked, "How did this dump come to be here?"

"Osage Indian," Stunted leered through his smashed face. "Heap oil, catchum many dollars. Build um brick tepee. Then Osage, him turn around and croak. Tepee, him go pot."

"You're quite a smart guy, ain'tcha?" Monk growled.

They unloaded beside the mansion. A lean, brown man stepped out to meet them, squinting in the headlights. He had a rifle.

"We got two visitors for the chief," said Stunted.

"The chief just left," said the man with the rifle.

"Oh," said Stunted. "So it was him in——"

The man with the queer eyes screamed, "Damn you! All the time about to let things slip where these guys can hear!" He slugged Stunted heavily with his right fist.

Stunted's face was already sore from the blow landed by the swarthy delivery truck driver. The new pain maddened him. He went down, but retained his grip on his rifle, rolled over and lifted the weapon.

Men shouted, and sprang forward to prevent bloodshed.

Ham kicked Monk on the shins. Monk bellowed in pain and knocked down the handiest of his captors.

"The house!" Ham yelled. "They'd shoot us down before we could get across the clearing."

The house entrance was not more than a dozen feet away. They dived for it. A rifle slug tore an ample fistful of splinters off the edge of the door as they went through.

Chapter 5

FLAME THREAD

THE door was of some rich dark wood. Paint had peeled off, but the panel still retained its strength. Monk tossed out one long, hairy arm and slammed it. Echoes of the slam echoed through the house, which seemed virtually devoid of furniture.

Monk snarled, "You didn't need to kick me!"

"It was a pleasure," Ham told him. "I mean—I had to get you in action."

"Yeah!" Monk hit a door at the end of the reception hall where they stood. It was not locked. Momentum sent him across the chamber beyond on hands and knees.

There was a table at this side of the room. It had been thrown hastily together from rough wood. But there was nothing crude about the apparatus on it. Black insulating panels, knobs, and switches glistened.

Monk veered for the apparatus.

Ham yelled. "That won't help us!"

"Heck it won't!" Monk began fumbling with the dials. "This is a bang-up radio transmitter-and-receiver."

"I know it." Ham was making for another door. "What good will the bally thing do us?"

"Bring help." Monk made a fierce face. "Trouble is, I gotta figure out what knob does what."

Glass crashed out of a window, a rifle smashed, and the high-powered slug clouted completely through the walls, missing Monk by something less than a yard.

"Take your time," Ham told Monk dryly. "You only have to get that thing working and call until you raise a station. Five or ten minutes should be all you need."

Two more rifle bullets came in, showering Monk with plaster dust.

Monk made another fierce grimace and gave up working with the radio mechanism. He followed Ham into another room—which held numerous boxes, all of them of stout wood, none of them bearing markings which might have hinted at their past contents.

Monk upset a box, found it empty, and began heaving the containers against the door to block it. Rifle lead went through the boxes with splintering ease.

"Them high-powered guns kinda complicate things," Monk grunted.

They retreated, finding an empty chamber, then one with cheap canvas camp cots on the floor. Blankets were piled carelessly on the cots. Odds and ends of clothing lay about. Cigarette stubs spotted the floor.

Monk scooped up an armload of the clothing.

"Maybe there's something in the pockets that'll tell us things," he said.

He carried the clothing as he lumbered in the wake of Ham. The latter peered through a window, rubbed dust off the pane, looked again, and began knocking glass out with quick blows.

"Sure, we can just walk away," Monk told him sourly. "They'll stand by and sing us a bedtime story, or something."

"Look, you accident of nature!" Ham pointed an arm. "There is a car behind the house, which we failed to sight before."

MONK looked and saw that the car was large and powerful; it was inclosed. He helped smash the rest of the glass out, let Ham jump down to the ground, then followed, retaining the clothes and grunting loudly as he landed.

They reached the car together and crowded each other getting inside. Monk threw his right hand for the switch, then made a fist of the hand and struck the instrument panel.

"Blast it!" he grated. "They *would* take the key out!"

He flopped down on the floorboards, tore a fistful of wiring bodily from under the instrument panel, took one rather long second in sorting them over, then joined the ends of two and the motor whooped into life.

"Handy to know how these cars are wired," Monk grinned.

The machine moaned and pitched in second gear, making an ample circle around the house. Ham drove recklessly, shoving his head up at intervals to ascertain their course. Brush switched the underside of the car. A loud clanking sound came from one of the windows, and Monk squinted at a spidery outline of cracks which had appeared magically in the glass.

"Glory be!" he snorted. "This chariot has bulletproof glass! There sure is a Santa Claus!"

Ham sat up, drove more carefully, and they pitched into the obscure roadway by which they had arrived. Ham was overanxious. He put on too much speed and the car skidded, went into a ditch and stopped. He looked outside.

"We can back out," he said.

Then he sat very still, for he had felt a small spot of metallic coldness come against the back of his neck. He had felt gun muzzles on his bare skin on other occasions.

"We should have looked in the back seat," he told Monk.

THE homely chemist reared up and peered around. The gun was removed from Ham's neck and shoved almost against Monk's flattened nose. It was a single-action six-shooter of tremendous size.

A young woman held the gun with one hand.

She was a lean, tanned young woman with a few freckles, not at all hard to look at. Her eyes were a rather enchanting blue, and she showed teeth which would have graced the advertising of any dentifrice. It was not a smile which showed her teeth. Rather, it was a grimace intended to convey fierceness.

"These are hollow-point bullets," she advised. "They would just about remove your head."

Monk swallowed. "Now, listen——"

"Shut up!" she requested. "I never saw you before, and don't know you. Maybe you don't know me. But you've heard of me. I'm Lanca Jaxon."

"Oh," said Monk.

"You've heard enough to know I'd as soon shoot you as not, or sooner," said the girl.

"Two-gun Lanca Jaxon," murmured Monk, who had never before heard of any young woman with such a name.

"A wise-cracker, like the rest of them," the girl said, frostily. "I never dreamed there could be so many alleged humorists in one gang of crooks."

Monk said, "Young lady——"

"Quiet!" she snapped. "One of these bullets won't be

funny. You two sit still. I'll get out and then you get out. I'll tell you what to do next."

She got out.

Three men came from the adjacent brush. Their arrival was so sudden that it was evident that they were men who had scattered to the edges of the clearing surrounding the house when the action had started, that they might be in a position to shoot down any one attempting to cross the open space. Each of the three held a gun.

"We'll take it over now, Lanca," one said.

The young woman looked at them very hard. She seemed to be trying to make up her mind about something of great importance. The gun was perfectly steady in her hand. She shrugged at last, and one of the men came over and got the gun she had wielded.

"You helped us a lot," he chuckled.

The girl said nothing.

Puffing and growling at each other, the remaining members of the gang arrived shortly. They surrounded Monk and Ham. Discussion followed. Three of them favored shooting Monk and Ham immediately. Others held saner convictions.

"Let the big boss decide," suggested the man with the peculiar-behaving eyes.

They walked Monk and Ham back toward the house.

The man with the queer eyes linked an arm with the girl, and said, "My dear Lanca, would you explain just how you happened to be in that car? And with a gun, too? It was Stunted's old six-shooter, wasn't it?"

The girl managed to say nothing in a very vehement manner. The man's eyes seemed to shift more queerly than usual. He conducted the girl into another part of the house.

Monk and Ham found themselves in the room with the radio apparatus. One of the captors went out, came back with a lariat of the cowboy variety, and they were bound with expert thoroughness.

"What'll we do with 'em?" Stunted asked, nursing his bruised features.

"I'll find out," said one of the men, and went to the radio apparatus. He switched the mechanism on. It was apparently of all-wave construction, because an ordinary broadcast program began coming from the receiver. It was a newscast. The commentator had a pleasant voice, rapid enunciation.

"—weird phenomena reported from various sections of the nation," said the voice from the radio.

The man at the apparatus started to turn knobs.

"Wait!" Stunted barked. "Get that!"

THE man reset the dial to the broadcast station.

"Some of the reports state that long ribbons of flame were seen in the heavens, accompanied by a weird crashing noise," said the radio newscaster. "Others insist they saw balls of flame. Astronomers, for the most part, insist that the phenomena witnessed are not meteors, as was at first believed. In no case has it been reported that a fallen meteor has been found."

One of the men laughed harshly, said, "It's got 'em worried."

"It'll have 'em a lot more worried before it's over," Stunted muttered.

"The last streak of flame in the heavens was reported over north-central Oklahoma and over Kansas," said the broadcaster. "This was hardly more than an hour ago——" The voice stopped coming from the radio. During the pause which ensued, crackle of papers in the distant radio station could be heard.

"Flash!" said the broadcaster, an undercurrent of excitement in his voice. "Here is an important item which just arrived."

"Aw, turn it off!" growled one of the men in the room. "Somebody has shot somebody else in Siberia or somewhere, probably."

Stunted snapped, "Nix! Get the news before we contact the chief."

They fell silent. The broadcaster was still rattling papers. He began speaking:

"It has just been announced that the explosion heard in downtown Kansas City, and which broke studio windows in this station, was a blast which thieves set off to enter the vaults of the city's largest bank," said the newscaster. "The raid was on a gigantic scale, and daringly executed. At least ten men participated. Bank officials have not been able to make a check, but estimate that the thieves could have escaped with nearly three million dollars."

Stunted seemed to forget all about his facial injuries. He grinned from ear to ear and slapped a palm resoundingly against a thigh.

"Boy, oh boy!" he chortled. "Get that! Get that!"

"Shut up!" some one told him.

They were all intent on the radio now.

"A few minutes after the robbery, one of the strange streaks of fire in the sky, which have so mystified the nation, was sighted," said the radio announcer. "Police are investigating a theory that this might be connected with the robbery of the bank."

Stunted said, "They begin to smell a rat."

"This concludes our news broadcast," said the loud-speaker voice. "We will be on the air later with more details of the sensational robbery."

One of the men shifted the radio control knob, *clicked* a switch and got down on short-wave bands. All of the men looked suddenly and extraordinarily cheerful.

The man at the controls made adjustments, switching on the transmitter. Then he picked up a microphone and a small notebook, evidently a code book of some kind.

"Calling CQ, calling CQ," he said into the microphone. "Station W9EXF, calling CQ."

Monk blinked as he heard that. It was the accepted manner in which amateur radio stations took the air and sought to establish connection with other amateurs. The "CQ" was merely the radio "ham" manner of stating that the station wanted to talk with anybody who would answer.

Out of the radio loud-speaker came an answer.

"Station W9SAV calling station W9EXF," the voice said.

The man at the apparatus grinned, winked. He consulted the code book.

"I have two headaches to-day," he said, obviously using the code. "How are you feeling?"

"The two headaches you were looking for?" asked the distant voice, which was somewhat distorted.

"That's the two," advised the man in the room.

"Have you tried diagnosing them?" asked the voice from the loud-speaker.

The man at the apparatus consulted the code book.

"Sure, I diagnosed them," he stated. "But they ain't the kind of headaches that tell you things."

Monk scowled darkly as he listened. There were thousands of amateur radio stations on the air all over the country, and a conversation such as this would not arouse suspicion. The code was simple, so simple that any one knowing it was code could guess what many of the statements meant. But a casual listener would not catch the hidden significance.

The radio conversation continued.

"You talked about a big headache that you felt coming on,

the last time we hooked up," said the distant voice. "Any sign of that one?"

"Nope," said the man in the room. "But I may get it yet."

Monk decided they were referring to Doc Savage.

"Otherwise, you are all well?" asked the loud-speaker voice.

"Nothing to complain about." The man at the transmitter hastily thumbed the code book. "How is your case of ptomaine—the one you got out of a can?"

"All cleared up," chuckled the radio voice.

Another look at the code book. "What do you suggest doing for my two headaches?"

"I'll see what the manual says," replied the far-away speaker.

The man at the transmitter laughed; then there was silence, during which Monk concluded that the "manual" referred to must be a cipher word designating the mysterious chief of the gang.

"The manual says to use two pills," growled the radio voice.

Grim expressions on the features of the men in the room as the radio conversation terminated showed Monk that they all knew, without referring to the code book, what a "pill" meant.

Stunted stood up, scowling.

"I don't like that," he said sourly.

"What's eating you?" the man with the queer eyes snapped.

"I ain't exactly a puritan," Stunted grunted. "But croakin' these two guys in cold blood don't come in my bailiwick. If they've got a chance—sure! But just to plug 'em, feed 'em one of them pills a piece, which we all know darn well is the boss's word for a bullet—not me!"

"Turned champion of defenseless manhood?" the uneasy-eyed man grated.

"Nuts!" Stunted glared at him. "I ain't forgot that pop in the kisser you give me, you cock-eyed gazoo!"

"Cut it out, you two!" a man barked.

Stunted continued to glare. The eyes of the other man crossed, uncrossed; then he shrugged.

"Aw, the delivery-truck driver getting away had me fussed up," he said. "I guess I shouldn't have smacked you."

Stunted said, "We'll let it go at that, then."

The man with the unusual eyes drew a revolver.

"I'll take care of the pill doses," he said. "I'm not as finicky as some."

He shoved Monk and Ham, propelling them before him through the door. They staggered about, helpless to do more than voice threats, which had absolutely no effect. The lariat bindings on their arms were painfully tight, securely tied.

One of the men left behind in the room called, "Say, what about that delivery-truck driver?"

"We'll look for him after I take care of this," said the self-appointed executioner.

They passed outside. The man with uneasy eyes did not close the door. Evidently he was calloused enough to want the others to hear the shot.

"Walk!" the fellow snarled. "You guys make one move and I'll let you have it here, instead of outdoors."

Monk and Ham walked. They could hear the tread of the man behind them. It was heavy, regular, betraying no nervousness, and there was in it the quality of doom.

Then the tread stopped. Monk thought afterward that there was also a faint gasp about the same time that the tread ceased. But he was never quite sure.

It was a long moment before Monk, apprehensive lest their captor shoot, turned. The homely chemist's little eyes flew round. His mouth came open.

The delivery-truck driver stood spread-legged in the passage. He had the uneasy-eyed man gripped by the neck with both hands. He held the fellow off the floor with an obvious ease, and the victim was making no outcry, hardly twitching.

Monk ogled the delivery-truck driver. The latter had changed appearance vastly, although he still wore the same garments and his skin and hair were swarthy. But the limp was gone, and the stature and fabulous strength identified the man.

"Doc Savage!" Monk gulped.

Chapter 6

TWO GENTLEMEN OF TULSA

DOC SAVAGE was not choking his prisoner, but rather, working on the back of the man's neck with corded bronze finger tips, seeking out certain sensitive nerve centers on which pressure, properly applied, would induce a state of paralysis lasting some time.

When the man was completely limp, with only his eyes and breathing showing that he still lived, Doc lowered him to the floor.

Monk and Ham stood immobile while the lariat was untied. Doc's finger strength managed the knots with ease.

"You hear anything that was said in that room?" Monk whispered.

"Practically all of it," Doc told him. "After using the ruse of the delivery truck I——"

"You sprinkled nails in the road?" Ham interjected.

"Exactly," Doc answered. "I hired the truck from a fellow who chanced to pass, and his clothing as well. He was carrying some roofing material, and the nails came in handy. The make-up material I always carry on my person. It was largely dye and wax for the cheeks."

Monk and Ham shook off the ropes.

"Where's my hog?" Monk demanded.

"Back at that old tank farm," Doc said. "I had to leave him behind."

Monk waved an arm. "What do you make of this mess, Doc?"

"Their chief obviously robbed that Kansas City bank," the bronze man pointed ut.

"Sure. But what about those streaks of fire in the sky? They've got a connection with the gang. And why'd they kill Willard Spanner? And who is that girl and what's she doing here?"

"Always thinking about women," Ham told Monk sourly.

"She acted queer," Monk said. "This whole thing makes me dizzy."

Doc picked up the gun which had been carried by the man with the roving eyes. He fired it twice. The reports were ear-splitting.

"To make them think you have been executed," the bronze man breathed. "That should give us a moment or so respite."

They eased back through the house until they encountered a door which seemed to be locked. Ordinarily, a lock offered Doc Savage few difficulties. But this was a padlock and hasp—on the other side of the door.

"We will try it through the basement," the bronze man whispered.

The basement stairs were behind an adjacent door and squeaked a little, but not too much, as they went down.

The room below had once been a recreation chamber and held a huge billiard table, the green covering mildewed and rotted. The table must have been too ponderous to move away. Adjacent was the furnace room. Grimy windows afforded faint illumination.

Monk stopped the instant he was inside the room.

"Lookit!" he gulped.

Two men were handcuffed to the pipes which comprised the heating system.

ONE man was long and lean, and his body looked as if it were made of leather and sticks. He grinned at them, and his grin was hideous because he must have had false teeth and was not wearing them now. His clothing was fastidious. When he tried to beckon at them, it was evident that the thumb was missing from his right hand, making that grotesque, too.

"I dunno who you are, but you look like angels to me," he said thickly. "You don't belong to this crowd. Turn us loose, brother."

The second man was a sleek, round butterball, entirely bald. Not only was his body round, but his head, hands, and his arms were like jointed, elongated balls. He wore a ring which had once held an enormous setting, but the stone was missing now and the bent prongs of the ring showed it had been pried from place, possibly without removing the ring from his fat rounded fingers.

"Yuss," he said, and his words were a mushy hissing. "Turn us loose." His "loose" sounded like "lush."

Monk lumbered forward, asking, small-voiced, "Who are you birds?"

"Leases Moore," said the leathery man with the missing teeth and thumb.

"Quince Randweil," said the man with the rounded anatomy.

"Oh!" Monk squinted. "The two missing men from Tulsa?"

Ham snapped, "It was Leases Moore's clothing that we got hold of in New York!"

Leases Moore made a leathery grimace. "How do I know what they did with my duds? They took 'em when they grabbed me and Quince, here, out of my car."

"A bulletproof sedan?" Monk demanded, thinking of the machine in which they had tried flight.

"Sure," said Leases Moore. "Are you gonna turn us loose, or not?"

Doc went to the handcuffs, examined the links, and found them of no more than average strength. The pipes formed an excellent anchorage. He grasped the links, set himself, threw his enormous sinews into play and the thin metal parted with brittle snappings.

"I'm a son of a gun!" Quince Randweil made it "gunsh." "That tells me who you are."

Doc said nothing. He finished breaking the cuffs.

"I heard them talking about you," said Randweil. "You are Doc Savage." The way he said it, the name sounded like "Savvash."

"We had better get out of here," Doc said. "We will try that bulletproof car again."

They moved for the grimy window.

"Why were you being held?" Monk asked Leases Moore.

"That," Leases Moore said promptly, "is the blackest mystery a man ever went up against. They wouldn't tell us."

"Ransom?"

"They never mentioned it."

"Know their names?"

"Only that runt Stunted," said Leases Moore. "I never saw any of them before. Neither has Quince, here."

The rounded man bobbed all of his layers of fat in agreement.

"What is their game?" Monk asked.

"Search us," replied Leases Moore. "That's another mystery."

Doc Savage was working on the window, and now it came open with only minor squeaks of complaint.

"Out," said the bronze man, and boosted lean, leathery Leases Moore out through the aperture, after first taking a look around.

Quince Randweil was helped out next. He and Moore ran for the car, which had been wheeled back into the clearing and stood not many yards from the house. They ran boldly, with more haste than caution.

"The dopes," Monk growled. "They oughta be careful until we get out."

Then his jaw fell, for Leases Moore and Quince Randweil had started the car and were racing wildly away, the engine making a great deal of noise.

"Why, the double-crossers!" Monk gritted.

THE homely chemist had one pronounced failing. When he got mad, he was inclined to go into action without forethought of the consequences. Now he gave every indication of intending to climb out of the window and pursue the two fleeing men.

Doc dropped a hand on Monk's shoulder and settled him back on the basement floor.

"Wait," said the bronze man.

Upstairs, there was excited shouting. They had heard the car's departure. Guns began going off.

"They may not see who is in the car, and think we have escaped," Doc said. "That will give us a chance to prowl about this place, and possibly overhear something that will give us a better line on what is going on."

There was a staccato series of deafening reports, undoubtedly the voice of Stunted's cherished automatic rifle from which the barrel had been bobbed. Six guns made noises more nearly resembling firecrackers, and a shotgun boomed deeply.

There was a general charge of men from the house. They had obviously found in the hallway the senseless man with the queer eyes. Their wild rage might have been ludicrous under other circumstances.

Doc had gotten the soiled cellar window shut. They watched the excitement from behind its semiopaque screen.

Monk grinned. "Wonder how many of 'em was around?"

"I was unable to ascertain," Doc told him.

"Looks like more'n a dozen pulling out after that car," Monk offered. "Bet they're all leaving."

Doc Savage nodded, admitting, "Now is as good a time as any to look around."

They left the basement. The stair squeaking as they went up seemed louder than before, for the house was very silent.

"I didn't see that girl leave," Monk whispered. "Maybe we can find her and ask questions."

"And probably get shot," Ham said pessimistically.

They listened. Outdoors, in the morning sunlight, birds were making sound. Wind fluttered scrub-oak leaves.

Then they heard a voice. It was a steady, well-modulated voice, and it came in spells. There was also an answering voice, this one metallic and difficult to distinguish.

Monk breathed, "The radio! Somebody is using it!"

They made for the room which held the radio transmitting-and-receiving apparatus. The door was open. One of the gang crouched over the mechanism, code book in one hand.

"So you think the weather should be warmer out in San Francisco," he was saying. "Yes, old man, that's probably true, and if, as you say, the manual says Frisco is a good place to be, we'll go——"

Behind Doc Savage and his companions, Stunted yelled, "Get them lunch hooks up, you three guys!"

Stunted, for all of his villainy, seemed to have some of the spirit attributed to old-time Western bad men. He disliked shooting down his victims in cold blood.

Had he, having come back unheard, or possibly never having left the house, started shooting without warning, Doc Savage or one of the pair with him, possibly all of them, would have died then. As it was, they reacted unconsciously to the command. They pitched forward into the radio room.

THE man at the radio apparatus cried out in excitement and went for a gun. He was infinitely slow.

Doc Savage, lunging across the room, sent out a fist and the man bounced from it to the apparatus table. His weight ruptured wiring, and sparks sizzled and blue smoke arose.

The fellow had succeeded in freeing his gun from a pocket, and it bounced across the floor. Monk got it.

Out in the corridor, Stunted bawled, "You guys ain't got no sense a-tall! Come outa there! This cannon of mine'll throw lead right through them walls!"

Monk lifted his captured revolver, then lowered it, grimacing to his companions. "Maybe he won't shoot if he thinks we're unarmed."

Stunted lifted his voice, yelling for assistance. He did not enter the radio room. His bellow was ample to carry to his associates.

The man on the radio table fell to the floor, but did not move afterward. A spot on his coat was smoking where it had been ignited by an electric arc.

Ham went over and rubbed the smoulder out with a foot.

Doc threw up the window, making ample noise for Stunted to hear. Then he listened. Stunted had fallen silent. Doc picked up a chair and dropped it out of the window. Hitting the ground outside, it sounded not unlike a man dropping from the window.

Stunted swore, and they could hear him rushing for the door which led outside.

Doc led his two men out of the radio room—not through the window, but back into the corridor which Stunted had just vacated. They found a window on the opposite side of the house. It was open, and they dropped through.

Some distance away, men were calling excitedly. They had heard Stunted's yell. The latter answered them, advising what had happened. Doc and his men began to run.

It was the bronze man's sharp ears which ascertained that Stunted was running around the house and would soon glimpse them. Doc breathed a command. They all three slammed flat in the coarse grass.

Stunted came puffing around the corner of the house, and stopped. His breathing was distinct, loud. He muttered in a baffled way.

Doc and his men were perfectly motionless. It seemed incredible that they had escaped discovery so far. But Stunted was certain to sight them. Monk held his revolver expectantly.

Then a clear feminine voice called, "Stunted! They went around the other way!"

Doc and his two aides eyed the house. The girl who had said her name was Lanca Jaxon was leaning from a second-story window, looking down at Stunted and waving an arm around the building.

"They got out of a window on this side," she cried excitedly. "They ran around when they heard you coming. Hurry up! They may be getting away!"

Stunted hesitated, growling. Then he spun and sprinted around the house, deceived by the girl.

THE young woman looked at Doc Savage and his two men. She could see them plainly, looking down from above as she was. Her arm waved sharply, gesturing that they should take advantage of the moment to escape.

They did so.

Scrub brush hid just as a flood of men poured into the clearing which held the strange mansion. Monk had underestimated the numbers of the gang, for there was nearer two dozen than one, and all were heavily armed.

"What say we stick around and bushwhack with 'em?" Monk queried.

It was an idea which Doc Savage seemed to favor, but which proved unfeasible, for the gang found their trail and followed it with a rapidity which indicated that a skilled tracker was numbered among the enemy. Doc and his men were forced to retreat, closely followed.

A small stream, rocky of bottom, gave them respite. They waded along it—first going up and making a false trail on the bank, then reentering the water and wading downstream. They turned back toward the house, confident the pursuers would waste much time untangling the tracks.

"That girl," Monk breathed wonderingly. "She helped us! But before, she stopped our getting away."

"You know," Ham said slowly, "it strikes me that when she held us up the first time, it might have been an accident. She might have thought we were with the gang."

"But what was she doing in the car?" Monk countered.

Ham shrugged. "I don't know. Possibly trying to get away herself."

Monk looked at Doc. "What about this girl?"

The bronze man said, "That is why we are going back."

Their flight had taken them almost two miles before they encountered the stream, and now, going back, they were cautious. They spread, separating from each other by the space of a hundred feet or so, in order that if one were discovered, the others might be clear to render assistance.

It was Ham who, some ten minutes later, stopped in a clearing and squinted intently. He could see a building, a large shack of a structure, through a rent in the scrub-oak thickets. The obvious newness of the building intrigued him. He veered over to find Doc.

He was surprised, and a little chagrined, to discover the bronze man had already sighted the structure and had climbed a small tree in order to view it more closely.

"Think it has any connection with this gang?" Ham asked.

"They have been around the building," Doc said. "All of them just went inside. They had that girl along."

Ham exploded, "But I thought they were tailing us!"

"They gave that up some minutes ago," Doc advised him.

The bronze man whistled a perfect imitation of a bird common to Oklahoma, giving the call twice. It was the signal which they had agreed upon to summon each other, and Monk ambled up shortly, his small eyes curious.

"That shed of a building," Doc told him. "All of our friends seem to have gone inside it."

Monk swung up a small tree with an ease that could not have been bettered by one of the apes which he so closely resembled. He peered for a moment.

"That thing don't look like an ordinary shed," he said. "It's kinda round, for one thing."

"We are going over to investigate," Doc told him.

The scrub oaks were thick, and down in a small valley which they found it necessary to cross, briars and small thorny bushes interlaced to form a barrier that they penetrated but slowly. On either side of the defile trees grew high, so that their view of the shed was cut off completely.

They were still in the arroyo when they heard a long, brittle crack of a noise. It was distinct, and very loud, with an utterly distinct quality. They had heard that noise before—in New York City, and in Oklahoma. It was a noise such as had been heard, according to newspaper and radio reports, by many persons in various parts of the United States. Always, it had been accompanied by threads of flame in the sky.

Doc and his two aides looked upward. There was no trace of a fiery ribbon in the heavens.

"Come on!" Doc rapped. "Let's get to that shed."

They raced forward. A moment later, Monk emitted an excited howl.

"That shed!" he bawled. "It's afire!"

THE shed must have been soaked with some inflammable compound, some substance which burned even more readily than gasoline, for it was a crackling pyre of flame when they reached it.

Trees, ignited by the terrific heat, were bursting into flame as far as a score of yards from the structure.

Doc and his men circled the spot. They saw nothing, heard no screams which would indicate human beings inside the burning structure. They would have been dead by now, anyway. There was nothing for the bronze man and his aides to do but to stand by and extinguish such of the flames as threatened to spread and become a forest fire.

Eventually, they went back to the house where they had been first attacked. Their attackers had flown thoroughly. The radio transmitting-and-receiving apparatus had been smashed. The odds and ends of clothing were gone.

Doc Savage had no finger-printing outfit with him, but managed to improvise one by employing a mixture of ordinary pulverized pencil lead and burned cork on white surfaces in the kitchen regions.

He examined these, using the bottom which he broke from a milk bottle for a magnifier. He looked intently for some time at the prints thus brought out.

Monk and Ham watched him. Both were fully aware of the facility with which the bronze man retained a mental image. They were willing to bet he could run through a finger-print classification days later and pick out any prints which matched those he was viewing now.

They searched for some time, but the house offered nothing more to solve the mystery of what was behind the murder of Willard Spanner, and the robbery of some millions of dollars from a Kansas City bank. Neither was there a clue to the meaning of the streaks in the sky and the accompanying cracking noises.

They went back to the shed, which had burned itself down. Poking through the hot embers was a procedure more fruitless than the search of the house. The incredibly hot fire had consumed everything inflammable, had melted together such metal work as there had been inside, making it unrecognizable, except for what apparently had been two large and excellent metal-working lathes.

"We're drawing blanks fast," Monk said.

Ham was sober. "I wonder what happened to that gang and the girl? Were they burned to death?"

Doc Savage said nothing.

They found the pig, Habeas Corpus, on their way back to Tulsa.

Chapter 7

PERIL IN FRISCO

THEY spent four hours investigating in Tulsa. Interesting things came to light.

The revolver which Monk had secured from the man knocked out in the radio room of the strange house in the brush, had been sold to Leases Moore a year previously. Further inquiry brought to light the fact that Leases Moore had purchased a number of firearms, revolvers, shotguns, and automatic rifles, during the past six months.

"Which makes me think of Stunted's bobtailed automatic rifle," Monk growled.

The house in the hills had been built by an Osage made wealthy by oil, who had later died. This fact, corroborating what the gang had told Monk, Doc Savage secured from a rather remarkable "morgue" of personal sketches maintained by a feature writer on the *Graphic*, a Tulsa morning newspaper.

The feature writer was a dresser whose sartorial perfection rivaled that of Ham, and he was a mine of information. It seemed that he kept in his morgue bits of information about all persons of importance in and about Tulsa.

Doc Savage was enabled, through the morgue, to make an interesting scrutiny of the careers of Leases Moore and Quince Randweil.

Leases Moore was a broker of oilfield leases; in popular parlance, a "lease robber." He had never been in the penitentiary. That was about all that could be said for his business tactics. He was sharp, squeezing and scheming, qualities, it seemed, which had made him a millionaire.

Quince Randweil had started life as a small-time gambler, had trafficked in liquor during prohibition, and had later taken over the local dog-racing track, a profitable affair indeed. He was also reported to be the undercover gambling czar locally, and not above turning a dishonest penny now and then.

But, like Leases Moore, he had never been convicted of a crime more serious than overtime parking, speeding, parking without lights and even jay-walking.

Of these trivial offenses, there was an incredible array of convictions. Doc Savage asked about that.

"The police tried to ride him out of town by picking him up on every conceivable charge," advised the sartorially perfect *Graphic* feature writer. "That was two years ago. It didn't work."

The really important development of the investigation came from the local airport. Monk turned it up when he perused the list of passengers taking planes that morning. He was excited when he got Doc Savage on the telephone at the *Graphic*.

"The Frisco angle is getting hot, Doc!" he declared.

The bronze man queried, "Yes?"

"Leases Moore and Quince Randweil caught the morning plane for San Francisco," Monk advised.

Doc SAVAGE did not hire a fast plane for the trip to San Francisco, as might ordinarily have been his course. There was a regular airliner due shortly, and it was faster than anything available for a quick charter. When the liner pulled out, he and his two aides were aboard it.

The plane had a radio. Doc communicated with New York, consulting his three aides who were there—"Johnny," "Long Tom," and "Renny." They had turned up nothing of importance in connection with the death of Willard Spanner.

At the first stop, Doc bought newspapers. There was much news concerning the flame streaks in the sky. Police were beginning to connect the phenomena with criminal activities, for in three distinct cases, in addition to the bank robbery in Kansas City, profitable crimes had been committed shortly before the weird streaks appeared in the heavens.

Doc and his two companions read the headlines while the plane was being fueled, and punctuated their reading with munches at sandwiches secured at the airport restaurant. Perhaps that was why they failed to notice a lean, neatly dressed man watching them.

The lean man was careful to keep his scrutiny furtive. He had boarded the plane in Tulsa, along with three other passengers in addition to Doc's party. He had two suitcases—one of medium size, one very large. He had seated himself well forward in the plane and had not once looked in Doc Savage's direction with anything bordering more than usual interest. He was doing his watching now from outside the airport restaurant window.

After the fueling, the man was first to enter the plane. He stooped over quickly, opened his small suitcase and took out an object which at first might have been mistaken for a bundle of tightly wound steel wire. He walked back and tucked this in one of the baggage racks where it would not be observed.

He left the plane, went hurriedly to the restaurant, and put in a long-distance call to an Arizona city. The promptness with which the call was completed indicated the other party had been awaiting it. The man consulted a code book.

"The weather is perfect," he said.

"Swell," said the voice over the wire. "We will pick you up, understand?"

"I understand," said the man.

He hung up, returned to the plane, and resumed his seat just before the giant craft took the air, motors making high-pitched sound outside the sound-proofed cabin. The air was rough, and the ship pitched slightly.

Below was an expanse of terrain not especially inviting to the eye, being composed mostly of sand and sagebrush, with here and there a butte, hardly impressive from the air, to break the monotony. The plane flew for two hours. The afternoon was well along.

The lean man stooped over and opened his large suitcase. It held a parachute. He had some difficulty wriggling into the harness, bending over as he was in order to avoid notice. When he had the harness almost in place, he lifted his head to see if he had attracted attention.

He had. Doc Savage was already in the aisle, and coming forward.

The lean man dived for the door. He had difficulty getting it open against the force of the propeller slipstream, but finally succeeded and lunged through. The face was triumphant. But the expression changed quickly. A hand—it felt like the clamp of some metal-compressing machine—had grasped his ankle.

The man cursed shrilly. He hung down from the plane, smashed about by the terrific rush of air, only the grip on his ankle preventing him from falling clear. His body battered the hard plane fuselage. Then he was slowly hauled upward toward the plane door.

Desperate, the man whipped out a gun. He was not unlike a rag held in a stiff breeze, and his first shot went wild. Then, grasping the edge of the cabin door, he took deliberate aim.

Doc Savage let him fall. It was the only move that would preserve the bronze man's life.

THE lean man fell away behind, turning over and over in the air. That he had made parachute jumps before was evident from the way in which he kicked his legs to stop his gyrations in the air. Then he plucked the ripcord and the silk parachute blossomed out whitely.

The plane was in an uproar. Passengers yelled excitedly and crowded to the windows on the side of the door, upsetting the equilibrium of the plane and causing the pilot to do some howling of his own.

Doc Savage lunged to the side of the pilot.

"Follow that man down!" he rapped.

Such was the quality of compelling obedience in the bronze man's remarkable voice that the pilot obeyed without stopping to reason out why he should.

Monk charged forward, reached Doc and demanded, "Why'd that guy jump?"

Doc Savage sent one glance fanning the horizon and saw nothing to cause alarm. There was no signal visible below.

"Search the plane!" he said crisply.

Passengers objected strenuously to having their baggage rifled, and there was no time for explanations. Ham lost his temper and knocked out a young salesman who tried to defend a stout black case which, when Ham opened it, proved to contain a small fortune in gem samples.

Monk lost numerous of the red bristles which served him as hair to a fat woman who had no idea of seeing her fitted case opened by the simian chemist.

The pilot still fought the controls. The associate pilot and the hostess trying to do their bit toward restoring calm, only added to the bedlam.

It was Doc Savage who found the bomb that the lean man had hidden. He smashed a window and heaved it overboard. Whether the missile exploded when it hit the hard earth below, or slightly before, was difficult to decide, but a sizable cloud of smoke and débris arose—enough of a cloud to prove that the plane would have been blown into fragments.

THE pilot had followed the man with the parachute only until the balance of his plane had been affected by the shifting passengers, and in the ensuing excitement, he had forgotten the bronze man's orders. The ship was now some distance from the parachute.

The white silk lobe was only a spot on the desert floor. It had settled into a canyon, they saw.

Doc advanced again and spoke grimly to the pilot, and that worthy, suddenly apprised of the bronze man's identity and shown a small card, hastened to send the plane toward the parachute.

The card Doc displayed was one directing all employees of the air line to put themselves at his service upon request, and had been issued partially because Doc Savage, a man of more wealth than any one dreamed, owned a goodly portion of the air-line stock.

It was impossible to land in the canyon. The nearest terrain for a safe descent was fully a mile distant. The pilot put his ship down there.

"Armed?" Doc asked the pilot.

The flier nodded.

Doc, Monk, and Ham raced for the canyon. It was rough going. Mesquite prongs raked their clothing and cactus prodded painfully. Once a rattlesnake *whirred*, and shortly after that Monk made a loud gulping noise and stopped. He said something.

Whatever he said was lost in a loud, rending crack of a noise which seemed to come from the direction of the canyon.

"There's that thing again!" Monk growled, and searched the sky in vain for some trace of a flame thread.

They ran on.

Then they heard the crack of a noise again, and once more listened and searched with their eyes. Again, they saw nothing in the sky.

The perusal of the heavens might have been an omen— they found no trace of their quarry when they reached the canyon. They did locate the parachute where it had been abandoned. Tracks in the sand showed where the would-be killer had fled. They followed these.

The tracks terminated in inexplicable fashion in the midst of an expanse of sand which bore every imprint with amazing distinctness. But where the tracks vanished there was a queer disturbance, as if a small and terrific whirlwind had sucked up the sand, then let it sift back.

Monk, frowning, insisted that some of the sand already floated in the air.

They hunted for an hour before they resigned themselves to conviction that, in some manner as yet unexplained, the one they sought had managed to vanish.

"This thing has had a lot of dizzy angles so far," Monk grumbled. "But this one takes the cookies."

Chapter 8

THE DEAD MAN'S BROTHER

IT was foggy in San Francisco. The air was full of moisture. The newspapers which Monk brought into Doc Savage's hotel room were soft with wetness. Monk seemed baffled, and he waved the papers.

"It's all over 'em!" he complained. "Here we've been in Frisco less than two hours and it's all over the newspapers. Now what I want to know is who told 'em we were here?"

Doc Savage said, "I did."

Monk shook his head. "But we generally keep out of the papers all we can."

"We have few clues to go on," Doc said. "None, in fact."

"Don't I know it!"

"So if these men come to us, even with the intention of getting us out of the way, it will put us in contact with them, at least," Doc said.

Monk grinned doubtfully. "Well, that's one way of doing it."

Doc Savage took one of the newspapers, but gave only brief attention to the story concerning his arrival in San Francisco. The item indicated, among other things, that the bronze man was on the West coast to investigate the murder of his friend, Willard Spanner. Or had there been a murder?

There was another story concerning the Willard Spanner affair. The newspaper publisher who had received the first letter demanding a money payment for Spanner's release, had received a second missive, insisting that Spanner was still alive and demanding money for his safety.

"This may be a newspaper publicity stunt," Monk suggested. "I've known some of the wilder papers to stoop to things like that."

Doc Savage lifted the telephone and got in communication with the publisher who had received the missives. Doc made his identity known.

"I would like to see those notes," he said.

The publisher tried to bargain.

"In return for them, you'll have to let us write up your movements exclusively in our paper," he said.

"We will do nothing of the sort," Doc said promptly.

"Then you can whistle for the notes," he was told.

The bronze man showed no emotion.

"Suit yourself," he said.

The publisher sounded less certain when he asked, "What are you going to do about it?"

"Tell the other newspapers what you are doing," Doc advised. "The fact that you are going so far as to block efforts to find Spanner, if alive, for the sake of a story, should make interesting reading. I also have a Federal agent's commission. The Federal authorities will be interested in your refusal of information and coöperation to an agent. I may think of other measures. For instance, the majority stock in your sheet is owned by a chain of which I am a director."

"You win," said the newspaperman. "I'll send the notes over."

Doc had hardly hung up when the telephone rang. It was the clerk downstairs.

"A Mr. Nock Spanner to see Doc Savage," he said. "Mr. Spanner says he is a brother of Willard Spanner."

"Send him up," Doc said, and replaced the receiver.

THE bronze man advised Monk and Ham that a visitor was coming up, and told them his name.

"Willard Spanner's brother!" Monk exploded. "I didn't know he had a brother!"

"He has," Doc said.

"Ever met him?" Monk asked.

"No," Doc said. "The brother is a military expert, and has been in China for a number of years."

There was a knock at the door, and Doc arose and admitted the visitor.

Nock Spanner was a hard-bodied man of more than average height. Although his hair was slightly gray at the temples, his age was probably not much past thirty. On his left hand he wore a rather large wrist watch, the band of which was composed of Chinese coins, linked together.

"I read in the newspapers that you were in San Francisco, investigating the mystery about my brother," he said in a crisp voice which held a hint of the accent sometimes acquired by Americans spending a period of years in a foreign land. "I just arrived this morning."

"Have you any idea why your brother was in San Francisco?" Doc queried.

Nock Spanner turned the wrist band of Chinese coins, which seemed to fit a bit too tight for comfort.

"To meet me, of course," he said. "We had not seen each other for seven years. I had finished my work in China and was coming back to the States to live."

"You have any ideas about this?"

Nock Spanner straightened the wrist band. "I have made enemies in China. I did not think, however, that they would strike at me through my brother."

"You think that possible?"

Nock Spanner shrugged. "I am at a loss to think of anything else. Of course, I knew little about my brother's connections in the States. He might have made enemies of his own. Or some one may merely want money. If so, I am willing to pay. Fifty thousand was the sum demanded, so the newspapers say."

"You have it?"

Nock Spanner nodded. He took a large automatic with a thin barrel from a pocket. Then he brought out a roll of bills, tapped them and returned them to the pocket.

"I can pay," he said. "But I want to know if my brother is

alive. I want the writers of those notes asked a question. If they answer it correctly, I will know my brother is alive."

"Is it a sure-fire question?" Doc asked.

"It is. I'll ask him my middle name, which I haven't used since childhood, and which I'll guarantee no one but my brother knows."

"All right," Doc told him. "The notes will be here shortly."

A MESSENGER brought the notes. They were printed on rough brown wrapping paper, the hardest kind of material to identify, and there were no finger prints on them. They were simple and intelligently worded, stating that Willard Spanner was alive and would be released upon the payment of fifty thousand dollars in small bills. The last line gave the method of communication:

WILL TELEPHONE YOU WHEN WE JUDGE TIME PROPER

"They're taking a chance when they use the telephone," Monk offered.

"They can call from some remote spot and depart quickly," Doc replied.

The telephone rang.

"Yes," Doc said into the mouthpiece.

"That newspaper guy said to call you," stated a voice which held a deliberate, artificial shrillness.

"About what?" Doc asked.

"About Willard Spanner," said the voice. "I'm one of the guys who's got him."

Using the hand with which he was not holding the telephone, Doc Savage made small, rapid posturing motions. Monk watched these, reading them—for the gestures were those of the accepted one-hand deaf-and-dumb sign language, and the homely chemist was being directed to trace the call.

Monk departed hastily.

"We have to know for certain that Willard Spanner is alive," Doc said. "It is reported that his body was found in New York somewhat less than three hours after he was seized in San Francisco."

"How we gonna do that?" the shrill voice asked.

"Ask Willard Spanner for his brother Nock's middle name," Doc advised. "The answer will tell us if he is alive."

"Sure." The other hung up.

It was some five minutes before Monk entered the room, wearing a downcast expression.

"Too fast," he said. "The connection was down before we could trace it."

"Instantaneous tracing of telephone calls is successful in fiction," Doc told him. "In actual practice, there are slips."

Nock Spanner had stood by, fingering the tight band of Chinese coins about his wrist during the last few minutes. Now he stepped forward.

"Just so there won't be any doubt," he said, and got a sheet of paper and an envelope from the room desk. He wrote briefly on the paper, standing so that none could see what he was imprinting, then inserted the sheet in the envelope, sealed it and gave it to Doc Savage.

"The name is written inside," he advised. "Unless they come back at us with that name, they haven't got Willard."

The telephone rang. It was the voice with the disguising artificial shrillness.

"The brother's middle name is Morency," the voice stated.

Instantly afterward, the other receiver clicked up. There had been no chance to trace the call.

Doc Savage opened the envelope handed him by Nock Spanner. There was one name printed on the stationery inside:

MORENCY

"Willard is alive," said Nock Spannner. "This proves it to me!"

JUDGING that there would be future calls from the men who claimed to be holding Willard Spanner—if, incredibly enough, he was still alive, as it seemed now—Doc Savage made preparations.

He got in touch with the telephone company and, after some discussion, succeeded in having the entire testboard crew set to work watching such calls as might come to his hotel. They were to trace each call instantly. With luck, they might succeed.

It was fully an hour later when the call came. The same disguised voice made it.

"You will take the money, get in an automobile and drive out of San Francisco on the main Los Angeles road," the voice directed. "Watch the fences on your right. When you see a piece of green cloth on a fence, throw the money overboard. We'll turn Spanner loose."

There was a momentary pause while the other took a deep breath.

"And listen, Doc Savage," he continued. "You're supposed to be a tough guy, but if you cross me, it'll be tough for you and Willard Spanner both!"

The other receiver clicked.

Doc Savage kept his own receiver to his ear, and not more than twenty seconds passed before a briskly business-like feminine telephone operator came in on the wire and said:

"That last call was made from 6932 Fantan Road."

Doc's arrangement for the immediate tracing of incoming calls with the telephone company, had worked.

Nock Spanner waved his arms wildly when the bronze man started for the door.

"But aren't you going to do what they demanded?" he barked.

"No," Doc informed him. "The voice on the telephone was not sufficiently anxious about the money."

Spanner blinked. "What do you mean?"

"I mean simply that the thing smells like an ingenious scheme to draw us to this 6932 Fantan Road."

Monk and Ham were following the bronze man.

"A trap?" Nock Spanner exploded.

"Possibly," Doc agreed.

"What are you going to do?"

"Oblige the gentleman on the telephone, to some extent," Doc replied.

Nock Spanner trailed along behind them, looking very uneasy.

FANTAN ROAD started auspiciously with fine mansions and new asphalt, but that was down in the five and ten-hundred-number blocks, and when Doc Savage had followed the thoroughfare out to the sixties, it had dwindled to the remnant of some high-pressure subdivision realtor's bad dream.

Finally, there was no pavement at all, and not much road, only two ruts in sand and weeds. Even the telephone line draped slackly from poles which were not all of the same length. It had been a long time since they had seen a house with a number on it, and just why there should be numbers on a dwelling out this far, without a rural designation attached, was a mystery.

Doc Savage made no effort to pull their rented car off the road, but stopped it and cut the engine.

Nock Spanner stood up in the seat—the car was an open phaeton—and peered about. The radiator made boiling noises.

"Darned if I see a house," he said.

"It should be less than half a mile ahead," Doc told him.

They left the car with its hot, sobbing radiator and advanced, walking through sand that repeatedly filled their low shoes, a circumstance which moved Monk to take off his footgear and pad along barefooted.

"The jungle ape in you coming out," Ham commented.

Monk only grinned and kicked sand back against the overlong snout of the pig, Habeas, who had paused to harass a large, black, frightened beetle. On either side there was woodland, the trees thick and large, sprouting from a mat of brush.

Doc Savage watched the road closely and discerned the prints of tires. They were not many. At one point, he noted in which direction spinning wheels had tossed sand. Before long, he had concluded three cars had traversed the road recently—two rather, for one had come and returned, and the other, its tires of a different tread and state of wear, had gone only one way. All of the tracks had been made that day. Night dew has a way of altering the appearance of a trail.

Doc Savage left the other three abruptly, without explanation, and went ahead.

"What's his idea?" Nock Spanner demanded suspiciously.

"He does that regular," Monk explained. "He's gonna look things over. We'd better take it easy."

Doc Savage did not follow the two ruts along the sand that was the road, but turned into the undergrowth and moved there. It was uncanny, the silence with which he traveled. There was no sign of a house as yet. But the telephone people had said there was a dwelling here, so there must be one.

The bronze man was traveling downwind from the road, and was scenting the air from time to time. Years of training had not quite given him the olfactory organs of a wild animal, but his senses were developed far beyond those of ordinary ability.

He caught the odor of tobacco smoke. He trailed it up wind, and if his caution had been remarkable before, it was miraculous now. He made no sound in coming upon two figures crouched beside the road.

They were men. They were arguing.

"I tell you I heard a car," one said. "It stopped down the road. That's suspicious!"

"You're always hearing things," said the other, sourly.

Possibly the hearing of both was a trifle deficient, for it was hardly reasonable that neither should know of Doc Savage's presence until the giant of bronze hurled down upon them; but such was what happened.

Doc had calculated his leap carefully and nothing went amiss. He landed with a hand on the back of each man's neck, and the shock of that drove them down, burying their faces in the gritty earth. They struggled. One man managed to bleat out a cry. He sounded like a caught rabbit.

Terrific pressure, skillfully administered, began to tell, so that the pair groveled with less violence, finally becoming limp and all but unconscious. Doc turned them over.

They were Leases Moore and Quince Randweil.

Chapter 9

MURDER SPREE

THE piping bleat—Quince Randweil had emitted it—had been loud enough to carry to Monk, Ham, and Nock Spanner, and they came up, running on their toes for greater silence.

"Ah, the two gentlemen of mystery," Ham said dryly.

"They were watching the road," Doc told him.

Doc Savage had not induced the remarkable paralytic state which he could administer by pressure upon certain spinal nerve centers, so Quince Randweil and Leases Moore soon revived enough to speak. They behaved in a manner somewhat unexpected.

"Boy, I'm glad to see you!" said Leases Moore, who had put false teeth in his mouth and now did not look unhandsome.

"You said it!" echoed Quince Randweil, making it sound like "shedd."

"Oh," Monk leered fearsomely, "so now you're glad to see us! Yes, you are!"

"Truly we are," lisped Quince Randweil.

"And why in blue blazes shouldn't we be?" Leases Moore demanded sourly.

"We made a bad move and we know it now."

"I see." Monk made his leer more impressive. "An explanation for everything, I bet."

"Nuts!" said Leases Moore, and began to look mad.

"Now, now!" Quince Randweil lisped excitedly and made admonishing gestures. "It will not do good to get all bothered. Of course you gentlemen are aggravated with us!"

"That's a mild word for it," Monk told him.

Randweil lisped on as if he had not heard, saying, "It was our rugged individualism which made us act as we did. Yes, our rugged individualism."

Individualism was a strange sound the way he said it. He made it, "inniwissilissim."

He continued, "You see, we were mad. *Very* mad. We had heard that our enemies were coming to San Francisco, to this house at 6932 Fantan Road. We overheard that. So, being very mad and wanting to get even, we came out here. But we have not been having such good luck."

Monk said, "It's a good thing lightning don't strike liars."

"You don't believe it?" Randweil sounded hurt.

"Sure I do," Monk replied, as sarcastically as possible.

Randweil looked at Doc Savage. "Do you believe me?"

Doc Savage asked, "By now, have you any idea of what is behind all of this—the murder of Willard Spanner, the queer streaks in the sky, and the rest?"

"Not an idea," declared Randweil.

"And that's the truth," echoed Leases Moore, rubbing the knob which was his missing thumb.

"Of course," Monk agreed, more sarcastically than before.

Leases Moore yelled, "It is, and all of you can go chase yourselves! I'm not a guy you can horse around!"

Monk looked at Doc hopefully. "Shall I do some of my exercises on this guy?"

Doc replied nothing.

Monk registered cheerfulness, told Leases Moore, "There'll be more than your thumb and teeth missing when I get through with you."

"Hold it," Doc said, "while I look around a bit."

THE bronze man employed his usual caution in advancing through the brush, and when he had traversed a hundred feet, paused and listened at great length, in order to ascertain if any one were approaching, drawn by the noise made when Moore and Randweil were seized.

He heard nothing suspicious.

Birds had fallen silent, quieted by the sounds of the brief scuffle, but now they became noisy. So furtive was the bronze man's progress that not often were the feathered songsters disturbed.

The timber became thicker, with less brush and higher, more sturdy trees. Underfoot, the brush gave way to moss and dead leaves. Ahead, Doc Savage caught sight of a building of some kind.

The crack of a noise came then. Its note was the same as on other occasions—sudden, strange, a noise unlike anything else Doc Savage ever had heard.

The bronze man whipped for the handiest tree. His climbing was amazing. He had picked a tree of somewhat thin foliage. A moment later, he was high up in it. His eyes roved overhead—and riveted there.

There was a strange thing in the sky. No ribbon of weird fire. It looked like a ball of some dull, glassy substance. In diameter, the thing approached a score of feet, and its surface was not all of the same obsidian nature, but freckled with lighter and darker spots in an even pattern.

The fantastic ball was hanging back where Monk and the others had been left. It appeared to be little more than a hundred feet up. Nor was it perfectly stationary, but bounced up and down slowly, as if it had just landed on an invisible rubber mat.

The thing was surrounded by a faint haze which resembled steam—and *was* steam, Doc surmised an instant later: water particles in the mist being vaporized against the ball, which had been made hot by its terrific rate of passage through the air.

The ball was an aërial conveyance obviously, a thing of new and amazing design, a vehicle along lines utterly at variance with those on which aëronautical engineers commonly worked.

Most surprising, of course, was the lack of streamlining to be expected in a device capable of such unearthly speed. It bore no resemblance to the fish-bodied conformation sought after by designers. It was a perfect globe.

There was an explanation, somewhat startling in its possibility. The planets in space, the stars, moon, sun, were round or nearly so, and this, some scientists maintained, was a result of the application of the mysterious gravitational forces.

Was some machination with gravity responsible for the amazing powers of this ball?

There was another explanation for the lack of streamlining, a bit more sensible. The ball seemed capable of moving in any direction without turning. Was not a spherical shape the most perfect attainable streamlining for a body which must move in any direction?

Doc drove a hand inside his clothing, where he carried a small, powerful telescope. But before he could focus the lenses, the amazing ball dropped with eye-defying abruptness, and was lost back of the trees. Judging by the swiftness of its descent, there should have been a loud jar as it struck, but there was no such sound.

Doc Savage released his grip on the limb to which he had been clinging. He dropped halfway to the ground before he grasped another bough, held to it long enough to break his fall, then plunged on to the ground. He sprinted through the growth.

At first, he was cautious. Then something happened which led him to surrender silence to speed. He heard a loud, agonized bawl; unmistakably Monk's voice. Some one cursed. Doc ran faster. He heard brush crashings ahead.

Then came the cracking sound. It was something different this time, starting with a whistle of something going with terrific speed—and the crack followed, long and mounting frightfully, then dying away, as if betaking itself into the distance.

At the first note, Doc halted, stared. His scrutiny was on the sky. He thought he saw something. He was not sure. If anything, what he glimpsed was a blurred streak which arched upward until it was entirely lost. It was no fiery ribbon, however. The bronze man went on, seeking the party he had left shortly before.

He found Monk, Ham, and Nock Spanner, but not Leases Moore and Quince Randweil. The first three were stretched out motionless in the brush.

THERE had been a terrific fight, judging from the violence done and the state of the victims. Monk had two ugly cuts on the head, Ham one. Spanner had evidently been slugged in the face, for his lips were stringing scarlet over the green leaves of a bush which he had mashed down in falling.

Doc Savage listened. There was a leafy shuffling, and the pig, Habeas, came out of the brush, looked at Doc with small eyes, then turned and went back into the undergrowth. There was no other sound. Even the birds had fallen silent.

Doc Savage bent over the victims. Ham was already mumbling incoherently and endeavoring to sit up. Doc gave attention to Monk, and was working over him when Ham's head cleared.

The dapper lawyer stared at the prostrate, apish chemist. A horrified expression overspread his features as he saw the gore about Monk's head wounds.

"Monk!" he gasped. "Is he dead?"

Doc Savage said nothing.

Ham staggered up and wailed, "Monk—is he all right? He's the best friend I've got!"

Without opening his small eyes, Monk mumbled, "Who's my friend? I ain't got a friend, except Habeas."

Ham switched his anxiety for a black scowl and came over and kicked Monk, far from gently, in the side.

"I was not talking about you," he snapped.

The pig, Habeas Corpus, came out of the brush again, looked at them queerly, then turned around exactly as he had done before and entered the brush.

Monk sat up and began administering to himself, and Doc gave attention to Nock Spanner, chafing his wrists, pinching him to induce arousing pain, until finally Spanner rolled over and put both hands to his bruised mouth.

The instant Spanner was cognizant of his surroundings, he whipped his hand from his mouth to the pocket in which he carried his money.

"Robbed!" he screamed. "Fifty thousand dollars! Gone!"

He began to swear loudly, his profane remarks growing more and more shrill and violent until they were almost the utterings of a madman.

"That won't help." Monk put his hands over his ears. "Besides, I ain't used to such words."

"My life savings!" Spanner shrieked. "And you crack wise! It's no joke!"

"With this head of mine, nothing is a joke." Monk growled. "Only, bellowing won't get it back."

Habeas Corpus came out of the brush and went back again.

Doc Savage said, "The pig is trying to show us something."

Monk swayed erect, weaved a small circle and fell down; groaning, he got up again. Nock Spanner stared, realizing that the homely chemist had been badly knocked out. For the next few moments Spanner was silent, as if ashamed of his own hysterical outburst.

They went through the brush slowly, for the three who had been attacked were in no shape for brisk traveling.

"What happened?" Doc Savage asked them.

"It was that thing in the sky," Monk said hoarsely. "We heard a crack of noise, and looked over here"—he pointed ahead—"and there it was. It looked like some kind of hard, funny glass——"

"A new and unique terrestrial space ship," Doc interposed.

"Yeah?" Monk frowned.

"Globe shaped," Doc elaborated. "It can move in any direction. It's actual propelling machinery, I do not yet understand, except that it is almost soundless."

"Soundless!" Monk exploded. "That crack of a noise——"

"Did you ever have a bullet pass very close to your ear?" Doc asked.

"Have I?" grunted Monk.

"What did it sound like?" Doc persisted. "Was it a whine?"

"Heck, no," said Monk. "It was——" He stopped, mouth open, understanding coming over him.

"Exactly," Doc told him. "A body moving through the air at terrific speed pushes the air aside and leaves a vacuum behind, and the air closing into this vacuum makes a distinct report. That accounts for the noise these terrestrial ball ships make."

Monk sighed mightily.

"Well, if a devil with two spikes on his tail had jumped up, we couldn't have been more surprised when we saw this ball thing, ship or whatever it is," he mumbled. "I was goggling at the thing when the lights went out for me."

"Leases Moore picked up a stick and hit you," Ham told him. "About the same time that Randweil struck me, knocking me senseless."

Nock Spanner chimed in, "And they both piled onto me. Randweil held me and Moore used his fist. That was the last I remember."

Monk said soberly, "Funny thing."

Ham snapped peevishly, "Everything seems funny to you the last few days!"

Monk shook his damaged head as if he did not want to squabble.

"When I was struck down, I didn't go out immediately," he said, speaking slowly, as if the information he were giving was painful. "I was in kind of a coma, or something. And just before I passed out, I'll swear that I saw the girl."

Ham demanded, "What girl?"

"The one in Oklahoma," Monk elaborated. "Lanca Jaxon."

"Hallucination," Ham said, skeptically.

"Maybe." Monk nursed his head. "But she was coming

through the brush with that runt Stunted. Then she turned around and went back toward where that ball of a thing had been hanging in the sky."

Doc Savage stopped. "It was no hallucination."

"I didn't think it was," Monk told him. "But how do you know?"

Doc pointed at the sandy ground underfoot. It retained the impression of a foot—narrow, high of heel, unmistakably feminine.

"I wish we could talk to that young lady for a while," Ham said grimly. "She could deuced well explain a number of things."

They caught sight of the pig, Habeas. The shote's enormous ears were thrown back in order that they might not be scratched by the thorny undergrowth, and if actions were any indication, he had been waiting to see if they were following him.

Nock Spanner said, "That is the most remarkable hog I ever saw."

"He's been trained for years," Monk grunted. "Say, that ball of a jigger was hanging over here somewhere."

They stepped forward more briskly and came out in what amounted to a clearing, although the place was furred over with short brush and tall grass. This growth was mashed down over a spot a dozen feet across, as if something heavy had come to rest upon it.

At the edge of the area where the brush was crushed, there lay three dead men.

Chapter 10

DEATH ZONE

DEAD bodies have a certain distinctive grotesqueness which indicated their condition, and these three were certainly dead. Bullets had finished one of them, knives the other two.

The knife victims were not dressed as expensively as the one slain by lead, their clothing being cheaply made, nor did they seem as intelligent a type.

Doc Savage and his aides had seen the two knife victims before.

"Members of the gang!" Monk exploded.

"Worthies who were with the crew in Tulsa, and in New York," Ham said more precisely.

Doc glanced at Nock Spanner. "Ever see them before?"

Spanner shook his head. "Strangers to me."

Doc Savage bent over the victims, searching, but with little expectation of finding anything, for he had already seen that the pockets were turned inside out, indicating the unfortunates had been previously gone over.

The garments of the bullet victim held no label. These had been cut out carefully.

There were labels in the clothing of the other two, and these indicated, not surprisingly, that the suits had been purchased from a department store in Tulsa, Oklahoma.

Doc returned his attention to the man who had been shot.

"Been dead at least ten hours," he said.

Monk and Ham showed no surprise at that until Monk, watching the knife victims morbidly, suddenly perceived that scarlet still oozed from their wounds.

"Hey!" he exploded. "These other two——"

"Were killed only a few moments ago," Doc told him. "Probably while that mysterious ball of a thing was resting here."

Doc Savage gave more attention to the body of the victim who had been dead the longer period. He unscrewed lenses from his telescope, and these served as excellent magnifiers; in proper combination, they afforded magnification which could be surpassed only by the more expensive of microscopes.

"Finding anything?" Ham asked.

Doc did not reply, and Ham showed no sign of being offended, for he was accustomed to the bronze man's manner of lapsing into unexplained spells of apparent deafness, usually when questioned upon points about which he had formed no opinion definite enough to voice, or when asked about something which he wished to keep for himself, possibly to spring later as a complete surprise.

Monk nursed his gashed head and complained, "So far, I don't make heads or tails of this. It's the dizziest dang thing I've run up against!"

Nock Spanner waved his arms and growled, "What about my brother? What about that house we came out here to investigate? We haven't done anything about that yet."

Doc Savage reassembled the parts of his telescope and pocketed it.

"We will have a look at the house," he said.

"If any," Spanner muttered.

"There is one," Doc told him. "I saw it through the trees just before this—interruption."

THE house was about what might be expected. It was old. Once, when this had been a more remote region, and before some over-enthusiastic real-estate promoter had gotten hold of the region, it had been a fruit ranch. It looked as if it had not been lived in for a year or two.

They came upon a path that lay about a hundred and fifty yards from the structure, and Doc Savage at once moved ahead, voicing no word of explanation. The others were too concerned with their own hurts to be overly inquisitive.

The path turned. For a brief time, Doc Savage was concealed from the others, and during that interval he went through some rapid motions. A bottle came out of his clothing. It held a liquid which resembled rather thick, colorless sirup, and he sprinkled this over the path.

The bottle was out of sight when the others came in view. They walked through the sticky substance on the path without noting its presence. Doc said nothing. They went on.

Behind weeds that grew thickly along the fence of what had once been a corral, they waited and used their ears. Monk and the other two heard nothing, but aware of the bronze man's super-trained hearing, they glanced inquiringly at him.

"Apparently no one around," Doc said.

They eased toward the house. Its decrepit nature became more pronounced. Portions of the roof had no shingles at all. Most of the windows were gone.

Monk suggested, "Wonder if we hadn't better scatter out, in case something happens. If it's a trap, we don't want 'em to nab us all in one bunch."

"Good idea," Nock Spanner agreed, and when Doc Savage did not veto the proposal, they separated, flattening out in the weedy cover.

"I will go in," Doc said.

He left the others, worked ahead on all fours, and gained the door. Only the top hinge supported the panel. No sound came from within. Doc entered.

Plaster had fallen off walls and ceiling and was in lumpy profusion underfoot. Powdered spots indicated where the stuff had been stepped on recently. Doc made a closer examination. Men had been in the house very recently. He went on to another room, equally as cluttered up, and stood listening.

There was sound now, rather strange sound—a faint, high-pitched singing noise. It did not undulate, but came steadily, proof that no cricket was making it, although the note did sound vaguely like that insect.

Doc whipped for the source of the noise—an adjacent room. The instant he was through the door, he saw what was making it.

A portable radio transmitter stood on the floor. It was in operation. Near by was another, slightly larger box of apparatus, and from that ran wires which progressed through cracks in the floor.

Doc hurriedly examined the second box. The workings of the thing were intricate, but not so complex that the bronze man's scientific skill failed to perceive their nature.

The box was a delicate electrical capacity balance, an instrument constructed to register, by having its capacity balance upset, when any new object came near it. It was merely a development of the old regenerative radio receivers which howled when a hand was brought near them—only this, instead of howling, actuated a sensitive relay which in turn set the radio transmitter to sending a steady oscillating signal.

Exactly such a device as this must have been employed back at the oyster plant in New York to detect the approach of Doc Savage. Here, it had served the same purpose, except that it started the radio transmitter in lieu of actuating some other signal.

Doc spun about, raced out of the room. There was furious haste in his movements. The instant he was outdoors his powerful voice crashed a warning.

"Get away from here!" he rapped. "It's a trap!"

Monk heaved up instantly from among the weeds. Ham appeared a short distance to his right.

They waited.

"Spanner!" Doc called.

Nock Spanner did not show himself. Doc called again. Only silence answered.

"Blazes!" Monk snapped. "That's blasted strange!"

"WHERE was Nock Spanner when you last saw him?" Doc Savage questioned.

Monk pointed. "Over there."

They went to the spot. There was a trail where the leaves

had been mashed down, the weeds crushed. But it only led for a short distance before it became difficult to follow.

"He was heading back toward the brush," Ham said dryly. "Now I wonder what his idea was?"

"Might have seen some one," Monk said, in a tone which indicated he doubted the prediction.

Doc Savage dug a small flat flask out of his clothing. It was filled with greenish pellets hardly larger than common rice. He began shaking these out on the ground, and the moment they were exposed to the air they began turning into a rather bilious-looking vapor. This was swept away quickly by the wind.

But the strange vaporized pellets did one remarkable thing to the surrounding growth and the ground: They brought out tracks—tracks that showed with a distinct, sinister yellowish tint.

Monk gulped, "Well, for——" He looked down and saw that he himself was leaving the yellowish footprints wherever he moved. Ham's tracks likewise showed. Only Doc Savage left no trail.

"A sticky chemical I let you walk through," Doc explained. "This vapor causes a chemical reaction which makes your tracks visible."

Ham clipped, "Then you suspected that——"

"Just a precaution," Doc told him. "Hurry! We've got to find Nock Spanner and get away from here."

They began following the remarkable trail which Spanner had unknowingly left.

"Any sign of Nock Spanner's brother, Willard?" Ham asked.

"No," Doc replied.

They were in the woods now, away from the corrals, the rickety sheds. The tracks became farther apart, as if Nock Spanner had started running here.

"Darn his soul!" Monk ejaculated. "I can't understand what got into him."

"Listen!" Doc ripped suddenly.

He said only the one short word, but it was hardly out of his mouth before their eardrums all but collapsed under a terrific, rending crack of a report. Instinct made them look up. Surprise put expressions of blankness on their faces.

A fantastic, glistening ball of a thing was suspended above them. It was not the same ball they had seen before. This one was smaller, its color slightly different. And stretching from it and away into the sky was a trail that might have been left by a fast-moving skyrocket.

The ball was hot. They could feel its heat against their faces—heat which undoubtedly came from the friction of the air against its shiny hull at tremendous speed. As gusts of particularly damp mist struck it, the gleaming skin threw off faint wisps of stream.

"Under cover!" Doc shouted.

They lunged under the trees, and a fractional moment later, the ball dropped, hitting with a pronounced jar where they had stood.

"Blazes!" Monk gulped. "It's a stout thing!"

The ball seemed to be cooling off rapidly—more rapidly than was quite natural.

"Probably has an inner and outer shell, heavily insulated against heat," Doc said grimly. "Otherwise, it would get too hot inside for human life, and that in only a short period of traveling. And from the way it's cooling off, I judge that much of the heat is absorbed by refrigeration from within."

The ball lifted slowly and hung suspended in the air, unpleasantly like a fantastic bird of prey.

MONK, scrambling through the undergrowth, rasped, "The darn thing is trying to mash us!"

The ball floated back and forth and, peering closely, Doc and his men discovered what might possibly be periscopic windows, showing outwardly as little more than big lenses, at various points on the skin of the thing. These were not in one spot, but were located on top, bottom, sides.

"Got eyes all over, like the head of a fly," Monk complained.

The terrestrial ship leaped to a spot above them. As it moved, it left a distinct trail of what resembled glowing red sparks.

"That explains the fire streaks in the sky!" Monk barked.

Doc Savage nodded. "The luminous particles are exhaust from whatever mechanism propels the thing."

"But some of the balls don't leave a trail!" Monk pointed out.

"Possibly more perfected specimens," Doc told him grimly. "They may have equipped some of the ships with digestors which eliminate the luminous exhaust!"

That was a rank guess on the bronze man's part, a guess which, later developments showed, was accurate.

Doc and his men began to run, seeking to keep under cover. It was difficult, almost impossible, for the woodland here was open, and the fabulous bulb sank itself in the trees and turned slowly, as if it were a fantastic organism, with eyes, brain, and perceptive senses all in its round, gleaming torso.

Then it lifted a little and drifted over Doc and his men where they had been spied out.

There was a clicking noise and a small metal blob dropped earthward. It thudded into the dead leaves and popped itself open not unlike a large and very rotten egg. Exactly the same thing happened a bit to the other side of Doc's party.

"Gas!" Ham shouted, then coughed violently, stood up very straight, grasped his throat with both hands and pulled at it as if trying to free something lodged there. He was still pulling at his throat when he fell over.

Monk tumbled over beside him.

Whether it was due to his superior physical resistance, or to the fact that he held his breath, Doc Savage was able to run some distance and probably would have gotten away, except that the gas seemed to be assimilated through the pores of the skin almost as effectively as through the lungs.

Doc fell down a full hundred yards from the others.

WHEN Doc Savage awakened, the voice of the short man known as Stunted was saying, "I didn't figure I'd live to see this day. I sure didn't!"

When the bronze man opened his eyes, it was to see Stunted standing over him, a sawed-off automatic rifle tucked under an arm.

"No, sir, I didn't think we'd ever get you," Stunted told the bronze man.

Doc moved his arms over an area of a few inches. They were limited to that motion by handcuffs, huge and strong, one pair with oversize bands located above his elbows, three more pairs above his wrists.

He shifted his ankles. There were three more pairs of manacles there, and his knees were roped together and the knots wired.

"We're getting cautious," Stunted told him.

Doc moved his head. Monk and Ham lay near by, both handcuffed, Monk with nearly as many pair of manacles as secured the bronze man. Neither Monk nor Ham were conscious.

"They'll come out of it," Stunted said. "That gas wasn't the kind that kills, according to what the chief told us."

The man with the queerly behaving eyes came over scowling, shoved Stunted away and said, "Still working that mouth overtime!"

Stunted glared at him. "My rope's got an end, fella."

The lanky man with the queer eyes ignored that, and frowned at Doc Savage.

"Where did Leases Moore and Quince Randweil go?" he demanded.

"That," Doc told him slowly, "is something I also should like to know."

The other blackened his frown. "So they were around, huh?"

"They were."

The man swore, and the nature of his profanity indicated he had lived some of his past on a cow ranch.

"The two locoed jugheads!" he finished. "We found two of our boys dead out in the brush, where one of the balls had landed. Leases Moore and Quince Randweil killed them and took charge of the ball, didn't they?"

"The thought has occurred to me," Doc admitted.

"Just the thing we've been trying to prevent!" the man snarled, and his eyes crossed horribly.

Doc asked, "Who was the third dead man? The one who had been dead some time?"

The other man opened his mouth as if, in his absent-mindedness, he was about to make a correct answer, then his eyes suddenly straightened.

"Never mind that," he snapped.

"Where is the girl?" Doc queried.

Stunted said dryly, "Them two skunks, Moore and Randweil, must've kept her alive. They would. Gonna use her the same way he was."

The man with the roving eyes yelled, "Looks as if only a bullet will cork that trap of yours!"

Stunted advised, "Any time you feel lucky, you can try to put the cork in."

Instead of taking up the challenge, the other wheeled and stalked away.

THE man with the uneasy eyes was back some five minutes later. He looked rather happy.

"You must have had a drink," Stunted suggested.

"Nuts!" The other grinned evilly. "I been in touch with the boss. We all get an extra cut for nailing our big brass friend here."

"When you bear such tidings, all is forgiven," Stunted told him.

"The boss is gonna handle the rest," the thin man said.

"What rest?" Stunted questioned.

"Doc Savage has three more men in New York," said the other. "Guys called Long Tom, Johnny and Renny. They've got to be taken care of."

Chapter 11

THE FARMER GAG

RENNY had big fists. A medical authority had once claimed they were the biggest fists ever known on a man, including those of the Cardiff giant. Renny was not a boasting man—except on one point, and that was the claim that there was not a wooden door made the panel of which he could not batter out with his fists.

Renny, as Colonel John Renwick, was an engineer with a reputation that extended over much of the world. He did not work at that profession much these days. He loved excitement, and to get it, he was a soldier of trouble in Doc Savage's little group.

Renny sat in Doc Savage's skyscraper headquarters in New York City. There was a newspaper on his lap. Under the newspaper and hidden by it, was one of the bronze man's supermachine pistols capable of discharging many hundreds of shots a minute.

There came another knock on the door.

"Come in," Renny invited.

The man who entered was a tower of bones. He blinked at the newspaper, then fingered a monocle which dangled by a ribbon from his lapel.

"Your demeanor instigates apprehensions," he said in a scholastic voice.

"Didn't know it was you, Johnny," Renny rumbled, in a

voice that had the volume of an angry bear in a cave. He pocketed the machine pistol.

The newcomer was William Harper Johnny Littlejohn, a gentleman with two loves—excitement, and big words. That he was considered one of the most learned experts on archæology and geology was incidental.

"Has Long Tom communicated with you in the preterlapsed hour or so?" Johnny asked.

Renny blinked. "That one got me."

"Long Tom called me," advised Johnny in smaller words. "He indicated he possessed information of equiparable import."

"I see," Renny said vaguely. "No, he didn't call me."

Johnny stalked into the library, appearing thinner than any man could possibly be and still live, and came back with a book only slightly smaller than a suitcase. He opened it and began to pore over the pages of fine print.

It was a book on the life habits of the prehistoric pterodactyl, which Johnny himself had written.

"Brushing up?" Renny asked.

"I left something out," Johnny explained. "A matter of ponderable consequence, too, concerning the lapidification, or progressive lapidescence, of the oval——"

"Spare me," Renny requested. "I've already got a headache. Any word from Doc?"

"No," Johnny said shortly.

The door burst open, admitting a pallid wan man who looked unhealthy enough to be in a hospital. He was hardly of average height, and his complexion had all of the ruddiness of a mushroom.

"Something important!" he yelled, and waved a paper.

He was Major Thomas J. "Long Tom" Roberts, electrical wizard extraordinary, and he had never been ill a day in his life.

THE paper bore typewritten words:

I know you're a right guy and know you're interested in This Willard Spanner killing. Go to 60 Carl Street and you may learn something. Be careful, though. I'll look you up later and if you want to do something for me for tipping you off, that's all right, too.

Buzz.

"Who's Buzz?" Renny rumbled.

"Search me," said Long Tom. "But this is worth looking

into, simply because the public don't know we're interested in the affair. This man knew it, so he must have gotten a line on something worth while."

"It's eminently plausible," Johnny agreed.

Renny, after making remarkably hard-looking blocks out of his great fists, grunted, "Wonder what kind of a place this Carl Street is?"

It was a swanky residential thoroughfare. They found that out when a taxicab carried them along Carl Street half an hour later. The street was lined with apartment buildings, and it was necessary to look nearly straight up to see the sky. The buildings looked new.

No. 60, when they passed it, was one of the most imposing buildings, its apartments having large windows, and there were two uniformed doormen under the canvas canopy, instead of the customary one.

"What shall we do?" Long Tom pondered aloud. "That's a large place. Must be three hundred apartments. And we don't know what we're looking for."

"Charge in and start asking questions," Renny suggested.

"Aboriginal reasoning," said Johnny.

"Sure," Long Tom agreed. "We wouldn't get to first base, and maybe scare off our birds."

"It won't hurt to take a look," argued Renny. "I'll turn up my coat collar and go in."

"Where'll you put them fists?" Long Tom snorted. "I'll do the gumshoeing."

They directed their taxi around the corner and got out. Long Tom stood on the curb, scratching his head.

"It's just as well not to walk in too boldly," he declared. "These birds may know us by sight."

A bright idea apparently seized him then, for he left the other two, dodged traffic across the street, and entered a telegraph office.

Renny and Johnny waited. Five minutes passed, and the waiting pair became impatient. They were on the point of investigating when a messenger came out of the telegraph office. He was directly before them before they recognized Long Tom.

"Gave a kid two bucks to loan his uniform to me," the electrical wizard grinned.

HE went into the apartment building carrying a telegraph company envelope which was empty, and when one of the doormen tried to stop him, he glared and said, "Nix! You guys don't gyp me out of the tip for delivering this!"

Long Tom walked on in, and over to the directory board which displayed a list of the tenants, office-building fashion. This last was an unusual custom for an apartment house, and a break for Long Tom.

Long Tom took one look; then he wheeled, walked out. Excitement was on his pale face when he joined the others.

"Guess what!" he exploded.

"Blazes!" grunted Renny. "That's some way to start out. What's eating you?"

"Willard Spanner had a laboratory and room down on Staten Island," Long Tom said. "The police searched it, but found nothing to indicate why he was murdered. Am I right?"

"Right," Renny boomed.

"Yet Willard Spanner is listed in that apartment house as having an apartment there," Long Tom advised.

Renny lumbered forward. "There may be something to this angle after all. What number is this apartment?"

"Apartment 2712," said Long Tom.

FIFTEEN minutes later, Renny and Johnny appeared at the service entrance of the apartment building carrying a large wooden box which bore the designation, "Apartment 2712" on its sides in black crayon. Their scheme did not go far without hitting a snag. It seemed that the apartment house had a service department which delivered packages.

"We were to install this thing," Renny rumbled, and tapped the box. "Don't bother ringing the apartment. We got the keys."

A service elevator took them up, and, grunting a little, they carried their big box down the corridor. They stopped at the door and listened, heard nothing, exchanged glances, then rang the bell. There was no reply.

From a pocket, Renny removed a sizable array of skeleton keys. These he had brought from Doc's headquarters. He tried almost twenty of them, and his long, sober face was registering some anxiety, before one of the keys threw the tumblers.

Inside was a modernistic reception room done in black and shining chromium. Renny eyed it appreciatively. He was a connoisseur in modernistic apartments himself, possessing one of the most extremely decorated apartments in the city.

He and Johnny skidded their box inside with little regard for the polished floor. They closed the door.

"Hello!" Renny called tentatively.

Only echoes answered.

They passed through the first door. If the reception hall had been modernistic, this chamber was an extreme in the opposite direction, being fitted up in early Twelfth Century style. There were great broadswords over the fireplace, the table was massive and hand hewn, and two suits of armor stood at opposite ends of the room. Mounted boar heads set off the scheme of decoration.

"Not bad," Renny said.

They advanced.

The two suits of armor moved simultaneously. Each turned a steel gauntlet over, revealing a small automatic pistol which had been hidden from view.

"You walked right into it," said a voice back of a slitted helmet.

Renny broke into a grin. It was a peculiar characteristic of Renny that when the going got tough, he seemed to become more cheerful. By the same token, when he looked most sad, he was probably happiest.

"You took a chance," he rumbled.

"Oh, we figured you wouldn't ring in the police," said the man in the armor. "Doc Savage's men don't work that way."

Four other men now came out of the rear regions of the apartment. They carried guns. Two of them searched Johnny and Renny thoroughly.

"Lock the door," one suggested.

A man went to the corridor door and turned the key, then came back juggling it in his palm.

"Get us out of these tin pants," suggested one of the pair in the armor.

This was done.

JOHNNY and Renny said nothing, but studied their captors, and the appraisal was not particularly cheering, for the six were not nervous, and their manner was hard, confident, while the clipped unconcern of their speech indicated that they were no strangers to situations involving mental stress. They were the kind of men who could be thoroughly bad; none of them looked soft.

"Well!" snapped one. "How do you like us?"

"You'd look better with a black hood over your head,"

Renny said dryly. "That's the way they fix you up before they put you in the electric chair!"

"Aha!" The man waved an arm. "He threatens us!"

Another said dryly, "We got Doc Savage in California, and now we collar these three. Strikes me we've about cleaned up our opposition."

"The boss worked a sweat up for nothing," said the first. "This Doc Savage wasn't such hot competition."

"It was that damn Willard Spanner," grumbled the first man. "He was tipped off about the thing, and asked to get in touch with Doc Savage. We had to smear him."

"It wasn't so much the smearing," the second man corrected. "It was the way we had to grab him in Frisco at noon, then croak him here in New York a couple of hours later, when he tried to get away."

The first speaker nodded. "But he had mailed all of the dope to his new York apartment, and we had to bring him here and make him get the letter for us."

Renny did not ordinarily show surprise. But now his eyes were all but hanging out.

"You came from San Francisco to New York in less than two hours?" he exploded.

"Sure," sneered the other. "Ain't it wonderful?"

"I don't believe it!" Renny rumbled.

Johnny put a question which had been bothering him. "Was this ever Willard Spanner's apartment?"

"Heck, no," the other chuckled. "We just fixed that up as a kind of sugar coating on the bait."

Then the man snapped a finger loudly. "Blast it! There's one of these guys loose yet! The one who looks like he's about ready to die. Long Tom, they call him."

The man who seemed to be in charge consulted his watch.

"We'll take care of him later," he decided. "They start unloading the *Seabreeze* in just about an hour. We'll have to move fast."

The men now began handcuffing, binding and gagging Johnny and Renny, working with swift ease, a hard tranquillity in their manner, as if they were perfectly sure of their ground and expected no interruption.

They were more than mildly astounded when Long Tom said, from the modernistic reception room door, "Everybody stand very still."

Behind Long Tom was the box in which Renny and Johnny had carried him upstairs—against just such an emergency as this.

THE six sinister men in the apartment had been calm before, and their composure did not desert them now, for they merely turned around, saw the supermachine pistol in Long Tom's pale hand, were duly impressed, and made no exciting gestures.

They slowly held their hands out from their sides, let their guns fall on the carpet, and raised their hands over their head.

"Hold that position," Long Tom advised.

He went forward and freed Renny and Johnny, who in turn searched their prisoners thoroughly, disarming them. The search was not as productive as they had hoped, the pockets of their captives holding nothing but money; the labels inside their clothing had been cut out carefully.

"Tie them up," Long Tom suggested.

This was done, curtain cords, wire off floor lamps, serving as binding.

Long Tom frowned at them, asked, "What was that I heard about *Seabreeze?* What's *Seabreeze?*"

"A race horse," said one of the men promptly.

Long Tom shook his head. "You said something about unloading——"

"Sure!" The other shrugged. "The horse just came in from the South on a train. We gotta unload him."

Renny boomed, "That's a lie!"

The man looked hurt. Long Tom lifted his brows inquiringly.

"The *Seabreeze* is a new ocean liner," Renny said. "I read about it in the newspapers. It comes in to-day, and there's a lot of gold bullion aboard. The stuff is being shipped over from Europe."

"So!" Long Tom glared at their prisoners. "What's going to happen to the *Seabreeze?*"

No one said anything.

"It's just a coincidence!" growled one of the gang. "*Seabreeze is* a race horse."

"We'll see about that." Long Tom waved at the door. "We're going down to the pier where this ocean liner is docking."

"Somebody's gotta watch these birds," Renny boomed.

"You can have the job," Long Tom told him. "You thought of it."

They argued briefly and it ended by them matching coins, in which procedure Renny lost; so, grumbling and looking very solemn, he took over the job of guarding the captives while Johnny and Long Tom went to the pier where the liner *Seabreeze* was docking, to see if it had any connection with the present affair.

Long Tom and Johnny were jaunty indeed as they rode down in an elevator and hailed a taxi in front of the apartment building.

They would not have been as cheerful had they chanced to note the actions of a man at that moment in the act of parking his car down the street a score of yards.

THE man in the car bent over hastily, so that his face was concealed, and when he bobbed up to watch Long Tom and Johnny out of sight, he held a newspaper before his features in a manner which was casual, but effectively shielding.

When the man got out of his car, he had a topcoat collar turned up and his hat brim snapped down very low. He walked rapidly and entered the apartment house, managing to keep his face averted from the doormen.

In his free hand, the man was carrying a small case which might have contained a physician's tool kit.

An elevator let him out on the twenty-seventh floor. He waited until the cage departed, then glided to the door of the apartment to which Long Tom, Johnny, and Renny had been decoyed.

The man opened his little case. First, he took out a rubber mask which fitted his face tightly. The thing was literally a false face, padded so that it now appeared that the man had bulging cheeks, a crooked nose and more than one chin.

The case also disgorged a tin can with a screw top, and a funnel, the lower end or spout of which was flattened out. The man inserted the flattened portion of the funnel under the door. He poured the contents of the can into the funnel, and the stuff, a liquid, ran into the apartment.

The man stepped back hurriedly, and it became apparent that he was holding his breath. He went to a window at the end of the corridor, opened it and stood squarely in the stiff breeze which now blew in. He breathed deeply.

He stood there fully five minutes, consulting his watch. Then he turned and went to the apartment door, drawing a key from his pocket. Fortunately, the other key had not been left in the apartment door when it was locked from the other side, so the man with the rubber mask admitted himself readily.

The stuff on the floor had evaporated. The man held his breath until he had opened the windows, then went outside and waited for the apartment to clear of the gas which he had poured under the door.

Renny and the rest of the men in the apartment were now unconscious.

Chapter 12

MAN IN THE RUBBER MASK

THE man in the rubber mask seemed to know a great deal about the effect of his gas, and how to revive its victims, for he went to work on the late prisoners, first unbinding them, and transferring a number of the ropes to the person of Renny.

It was not long before inhalation of certain bottled compounds caused the men to blink and moan themselves awake. The masked man shook one of them violently.

"What happened?" he snapped.

The sound of the voice—it was not a particularly unusual voice, yet distinctive enough to be readily recognized—snapped the man who heard it into wide wakefulness.

"The big chief!" he exploded. "But what're you wearin' that mask for? You look like a goblin!"

The man in the mask ripped out, "I asked you what happened here! I didn't ask for any wise-guy stuff!"

The story of the raid by Doc Savage's three men came out—the narrators doing their best to gloss over the parts unfavorable to themselves, but, judging from the angry snorts of their leader, not succeeding very well.

"Fools!" the man yelled. "You do things just like a herd of donkeys! Where did Johnny and Long Tom go?"

The one telling the bad news looked as if he had found a worm in his apple. He hesitated. He had neglected to tell about the *Seabreeze* slip.

"It's bad," he groaned, and told the rest of it.

The masked leader proceeded to have something approaching a tantrum. He swore, and kicked those who were just regaining consciousness, so that they awakened more hurriedly and scrambled erect to get the more sensitive portions of their anatomy out of foot reach.

"You bunch of nitwits!" the man choked. "You should have told me that first! It may be too late now."

He charged into another room, grabbed a telephone, and could be heard snapping the dialing device around madly. When he got his number his voice dropped. Those in the other room did not hear a word he said, except for a final sentence which showed the man had been speaking in the strange private code which the gang employed.

"The cake should be baked half an hour earlier," was his last sentence.

He came back into the room looking somewhat less mad than before, and said, "Maybe I managed to get the bacon out of the fire."

"How?" he was asked.

"I contacted the boys and told them to go through with it half an hour earlier than planned." He consulted his watch. "That means right away. They may get it done before Johnny and Long Tom arrive on the scene."

The man eyed his watch again. "Half an hour should see the job done."

AT about the same moment, Long Tom was examining a thin wafer of a watch which had cost the electrical society which had presented it to him a small fortune. "We won't make that pier much before the half hour," he said to Johnny.

However, they had secured a driver who was willing to take chances, and by stopping a traffic policeman and exhibiting their police commissions—they, too, held them, as well as did Doc Savage—they persuaded the officer to ride the running board.

The results were remarkable. Traffic split for them. Their horn blasted steadily. They chopped fifteen minutes from Long Tom's time estimate.

"There's the pier," Long Tom advised.

Johnny craned his long neck.

"The situation has certain aspects of a premonstration," he said.

Long Tom looked puzzled. "A what, did you——"

From ahead came a sound as if a snare drum had been beaten hard for a short interval. The driver stopped the cab so suddenly that the wheels skidded. He heaved out of the seat, took a good look.

There was a crowd ahead, an excited crowd. At the snare-drum sound, the crowd showed an abrupt tendency to leave the vicinity. Many policemen were running about. Police-car sirens made an unholy music.

"This is as far as I go," the taxi driver advised. "There's a young war ahead!"

Johnny and Long Tom were already getting out of the machine. They forgot to pay the driver, and he in turn did not think of collecting. They ran forward. Men and women passed them. Two men led a woman who was having hysterics.

"They killed fifty men or more!" the woman screamed. "The bodies were everywhere!"

Johnny registered incredulity, and gasped, "A Brobdingnagian exaggeration, let us hope."

The snare-drum sound—surely a machine gun—rattled out again. Smaller firearms cracked. Shotguns went off. Gas bombs made rotten-egg noises.

A burly policeman loomed up and yelled, "Hey, this ain't no show! Get back where it's safe!"

Long Tom and Johnny showed their police-commission cards.

"What's going on?" the feeble-looking electrical wizard asked.

"Pirates!" said the officer. "They're cleaning out the *Seabreeze!*"

Going on, Long Tom and Johnny rounded the corner and came upon a surprising sight.

THREE very large trucks were backed up to the pier at which the bright, new liner *Seabreeze* was tied. The van body of the outer truck had been shot away over a small area, and it was evident that the interior was lined with thick steel. The truck tires were ragged where bullets had struck, but had not gone flat, indicating they were of solid rubber.

The engine hoods and radiators also seemed to be armored, although the engines were of a type which sat inside the cabs, and thus were difficult to shoot into.

A man—probably a news photographer—was getting pictures on top of a near-by building. A machine gun snarled from behind one of the trucks, and he dashed for cover. A fresh burst of firing started.

Possibly fifty policemen were in sight. Others were arriving. They had set up a regulation Lewis gun, and its drumming uproar burst out.

Johnny got his bony length down behind a row of parked cars. Windows were shot from some of the cars. Trailed closely by Long Tom, he worked to the side of a police sergeant. He asked questions.

"The *Seabreeze* is carrying gold bullion," the officer explained. "They're looting her. Must be thirty or more of them."

The sergeant drew the pin of a gas bomb, drew back and hurled it.

"Won't do any good," he added. "Them birds are wearing masks."

"Using regular army tactics," Long Tom growled.

"We'll get 'em," said the cop. "We got men taking their pictures with telephoto lenses. We're blocking every street leading away from here."

It became evident that the ship raiders had thrown up a barricade of sand bags, probably unloaded from the trucks, behind which they could crawl to load the trucks. Only rarely did one of them show himself above the barrier. Each lapse of this kind drew a fusillade of bullets.

Long Tom unlimbered his machine pistol, as did Johnny. They joined the police besiegers. There was little else they could do.

"Consummately unbelievable," said Johnny, referring to the whole affair.

"It does seem to be about as big a thing as was ever pulled in New York," Long Tom agreed. "Hey! Something's gonna happen!"

The truck engines had been turning over steadily. Now they roared. The huge vehicles began to move.

This was the signal for the police. Everywhere, officers leaped up, emptying their guns. Crash and roar of firearms was terrific. Bits of siding fell off the trucks.

The giant vehicles did not turn up or down the street, as expected. They continued straight across the wide waterfront thoroughfare. They were aiming for a large wooden door in a building. The first truck hit the door. It was of very thin wood, and caved in. The truck vanished inside. The others followed.

AN instant later, it was evident that a stout steel door had been put up from the inside of the building in place of the wooden one. A great roar of gunfire came from the building as bricks fell out of the walls here and there, exposing loopholes obviously prepared aforehand.

The police retreated. Occasionally, one fell, wounded.

The officers began to yell for ladder wagons from the fire department, in order that they might scale the roofs of the buildings.

"There's a court behind that building," a bluecoat shouted. "Try to get into that!"

"They're trying," he was informed. "The gang has the walls covered."

Some fifteen minutes passed. The vicinity began to take on the aspect of a battlefield. Out in the bay a tugboat maneuvered, a light field gun, secured from the fort in the bay, on its after deck. Police in number had grown to several hundred. White-clad ambulance attendants were thick.

Then something happened that knocked every one speechless. There was a rending crack—it really started with a whistle that might have been made by some body going at terrific speed. The throng gazed, stupefied, at the sky, scarcely believing what they saw.

"A big ball!" a cop gasped. "It come up out of the court behind that building and went away so fast you danged near couldn't see it!"

WHILE they still goggled at the heavens, there was another echoing report, and a second ball sailed upward, visible at first, but rapidly gathering speed until it could hardly be followed with the eye.

No more balls arose. Shooting from the building had stopped. Policemen stormed the place.

"They'll find exactly nothing, is my guess," Long Tom prophesied.

He was right. The officers found the trucks, badly riddled. They found one bar of gold which had somehow been overlooked in the excitement. Considering the magnitude of the theft, and the roaring manner in which it had been executed, it was remarkable that only one gold bar had been overlooked.

Six million dollars had been taken. The *Seabreeze* purser gave out that information. Not quite a dozen men had been killed, although one excited tabloid newspaper placed the estimate at two hundred. Altogether, it was the most spectacular bit of news which New Yorkers had experienced in a long period.

Most stunning of all, perhaps, was the manner in which the thieves had vanished. When last seen, they were fast-traveling specks in the sky. Nor was another trace of them discovered.

Of course, every one now connected the streaks in the sky—at first thought to be peculiar comets—with the mysterious balls. There was one point which caused confusion. At first, the balls had made streaks in the sky. Now they made none.

Long Tom and Johnny discussed that as they rode uptown, baffled and a little sheepish because they had been of practically no assistance in preventing the robbery.

"I don't understand it," Long Tom said. "Maybe the streaks weren't made by balls, after all. And what kind of things are these balls, anyway? How do they work?"

They got out of their cab in front of the apartment building where they had left Renny guarding the prisoners. Paying the fare took a few moments. They turned to go in.

"Look!" Long Tom exploded.

Renny sat in a car across the street; his head and shoulders showed plainly, so that there was no doubt about it being Renny.

"What the heck's he doing down here?" Long Tom quipped.

The next instant, one of Renny's huge hands lifted and beckoned to them, indicating that they should come over.

They ran across the street, unsuspecting, hands far from the armpit holsters which held their supermachine pistols.

Two men came from behind a parked car on the right. They flourished revolvers. Three came from the left, also with guns. They were members of the gang who had been in the apartment.

They said nothing. They did not need to, for their manner was fully explanatory of their intentions. Long Tom and Johnny put their hands up.

A small man got up from the floor of the car beside Renny. Crouched down there, out of sight, he had grasped Renny's arm and waved one of the engineer's big hands, thus giving the summons which had deceived Long Tom and Johnny.

Renny, it became apparent, was unconscious.

THE gang was using three cars, all large sedans of somber color. In not more than twenty seconds after the first man with a gun had appeared, the cars were in motion—Long Tom in one, Johnny in the other.

A woman had been hanging with her head out of a near-by window. Now she began to scream. Her shrieks were so piercing that a baby in a perambulator up the street burst into loud crying.

One of the men stuck a gun out of a car window. The weapon sent thunder along the street. The woman's head disappeared.

Another man in the car snarled, "We ain't killing women, you louse!"

"Who's killing women?" the other snorted. "I shot out a window twenty feet from where she had her head!"

The cars did not travel swiftly enough to attract attention. After a dozen blocks, they stopped in an alley. No one was in sight. A shift was made to three other cars of entirely different color and model. These separated.

Long Tom squirmed about as they began to bind his arms securely with bits of cotton rope. There was little he could do.

"What are you going to do with us?" he demanded.

"Plenty," a man informed him.

Long Tom managed to grab a wrist and twist it, causing the victim to cry out in pain, and, as he flounced about, his gun was dislodged from his waistband, where he had stuffed it.

Long Tom had been contriving at that. He tried mightily to get the gun. They beat him down and kicked him soundly for the trouble he was causing.

A long time later, the car stopped in a woodland. Long Tom peered out and discovered that the other two machines had also arrived by other routes. Far away, through the trees, the electrical wizard caught sight of a gleaming object.

"What next?" asked one of the men.

"The chief says to get Doc Savage and all of his men together," replied the man in charge.

"Risky, ain't it?"

The other shrugged. "We're going to do some tall question asking. Chief wants to know just how much Doc Savage has learned about us, and whether he has left a written record of what he has dug up."

Squinting at the gleaming thing through the trees, Long Tom suddenly decided it was a ball—a large globe of some obsidian material.

One of the men came over, took a bottle and a handkerchief from his pocket, poured some of the contents of the bottle on the handkerchief and suddenly pounced upon Long

Tom, clamping the saturated cloth to the electrical expert's nostrils.

Long Tom held his breath as long as possible, but they punched him in the stomach until he had to take air.

The first whiff brought the odor of chloroform. He coughed, flounced. He managed to get a lungful of fresh air. Endeavoring to make them think he had succumbed, he tried to fake oncoming unconsciousness while holding his breath again.

"Full of tricks, ain't you?" snarled the man, and hit him just above the belt.

Long Tom inhaled the anæsthetic in gobbling haste, and, before long, felt it take hold. His last impression was that of Johnny and Renny fighting against handkerchiefs being pressed against their nostrils.

Chapter 13
SINISTER ORGANIZATION

THE room was dark, so very dark that it seemed filled with something solid. At one point only did a trace of light show, a small faint glow which, on closer examination, would have been ascertained to be the luminous dial of a wrist watch.

After a while, there was noise of a door opening, and a flashlight lunged out whitely, picking up a prone figure. The beam collapsed. The motion of the watch-dial light patch indicated the man was being lifted and borne into another room, equally dark, but into which jangling sound of a radio speaker penetrated. He was dropped heavily, and those who had borne him stalked out.

Doc Savage's trained voice asked, "Who is it?"

The man who had just been carried in said, "Nock Spanner."

From elsewhere in the room, Monk's small voice spoke up, "How did they get you? And why'd you run off from us at that old ranch?"

"Oh, that?" Nock Spanner made a disgusted noise. "I saw somebody and followed them. At first, I wasn't sure it was some one. You see, I just saw a movement. Then, when I did make sure it was some one skulking, it was too late to turn back and get you. I wish I had. They grabbed me a little later."

Ham said from close by, "I am getting very tired of this."

Nock Spanner asked, "You all tied up?"

"Like mummies," Monk growled. "And handcuffs galore."

The radio ground out music steadily.

"What do you think they'll do with us?" Nock Spanner asked.

"No idea," said Monk.

"Have you—learned if my brother is still alive?" Spanner questioned.

Monk hesitated, then admitted, "No."

The radio stopped jangling music; there was a station announcement, then a news broadcaster with a staccato manner of speaking took over the microphone.

"Our affair of the flaming comets seems to be taking on the complexion of one of the most gigantic criminal rings of all time," he said, the radio loud-speaker reproducing each word distinctly. "At least half a dozen crimes of importance can be attributed to the Comet Gang so far to-day, the largest being the fantastic robbery of bullion from a ship at a New York City pier, only a short time ago. In addition to this, a jewelry concern was rifled in Chicago, and banks robbed in various other cities. In each case, it is certain that the robbers were members of what is now being called the Comet Gang, and escaped in the fantastic ball vehicles, which scientists admit to be some new type of terrestrial ship capable of traveling at terrific speed, and of handling with remarkable facility."

The radio commentator went on, and his broadcast became dryer and dryer as he ran out of concrete information and began generalizing.

"He's been on the air steady, pretty near," Monk grumbled. "Boy, am I getting tired of that voice!"

Nock Spanner said, "It is evident that we are entangled with a gigantic criminal ring which has perfected this terrestrial ship, or whatever you would call it, and are using it as a get-away vehicle in the commission of huge crimes."

The radio in the other room suddenly went silent.

"They cut the speaker into their private transmitter-and-receiver hookup when they communicate with each other," Monk said in a stage whisper. "Listen to what they say. They've sure got an organization!"

SHORTLY afterward, the radio in the next room went into operation. Evidently a call had been picked up on a supplementary receiver, and the large speaker cut in for convenience in operation.

"This is W2OLA coming back at my friend in California," said the faint speaker voice. "This is W2OLA in Corona, Long Island, New York City, coming back to California. I just got all of the tubes in the box, old man. Your system for doing it worked splendidly. All three tubes are thoroughly boxed. Yes, sir. I am going to deliver them now. So long—and seventy-threes, old man."

That was all from the radio.

Monk muttered in the darkness. "I'm getting able to pick out the general meaning of their code," he grumbled. "Take that conflab just now. It meant they've got something done in New York, something involving three——"

He left the words hanging. Silence was thick. The ticking of the watch with the luminious dial was audible.

"Go ahead—say it," Ham suggested. "That radio talk might have referred to Renny, Long Tom and Johnny."

"Yeah," said Monk, "that's what I was thinking."

Nock Spanner snarled, "Ain't there any way of getting out of this?"

"I wouldn't worry too much," Monk told him.

Spanner swore joyfully. "Then you have a plan?"

"No," Monk told him. "But Doc, here, is something of a magician."

Spanner muttered, "If the police only knew where to look for us. Why in Sam Hill didn't we leave a note or something, telling what we had learned, or what we intended to do?"

Monk advised, "Like lots of good ideas, that one comes too late."

Time passed. It could not have been much more than an hour and a half. They heard a cracking noise characteristic to the arrival, departure, or passage of one of the mysterious aërial globes. Then there came a voice.

There was something familiar about the voice. It took them a moment to place it. Then Ham gasped incredulously.

"That voice—the same one was on the radio from New York not over two hours ago!" he said sharply.

No one said anything for a while; then they heard the voice of the newcomer again, and within a few moments, other voices and the tramp of feet. These approached. Scuffling quality indicated men carrying heavy burdens. They came inside.

They bore Johnny, Long Tom, and Renny, all of whom were unconscious. The trio were deposited in the darkness.

"You birds enjoy yourselves," a voice said. "We're going to hold a party later."

The men departed.

Doc Savage heaved up and strained mightily against the handcuffs which held his wrists. There was no hope of breaking them. It was doubtful if, even with his incalculable strength, he could have broken one of them, for they were very heavy.

And three manacles held his arms. In addition, there were many turns of rope. It was against this that he struggled, and he was loosening it, getting a little play into his arms.

A stirring indicated that either Johnny, Long Tom, or Renny was reviving. It was Johnny's voice which first broke the silence.

"I'll be superamalgamated!" he mumbled.

The word was a favorite of Johnny's. He used it to express disgust, despair, surprise, or any other violent emotion.

"Feel all right?" Doc asked.

The ropes on the bronze man's arms had loosened somewhat, enabling him, by squirming mightily, to reach the row of buttons on the front of his coat. He tore one of these off, got it between his fingers, slipped it down between his manacled ankles, and began to work with it.

Johnny mumbled gloomily, "I feel like a valetudinarian."

"A man who can think of a word like that can't be so bad," Monk told him.

Doc Savage had managed to unscrew one half of the button from the other half; a threaded joint permitted this, although so skillfully done that no casual examination would have disclosed it. He carefully tilted the button and let the stuff in the hollow interior trickle on the handcuff links. He did this most painstakingly.

Nock Spanner growled hopelessly, "Isn't there some chance for us?"

Long Tom and Renny had both regained their senses now. Voices anxious, they made sure Doc and the others were unharmed. They noted the luminous dial of Nock Spanner's watch and asked the time. He told them.

"Holy cow!" Renny boomed. "We were brought from New York out here to California in not much more than two hours!"

Nock Spanner demanded desperately, "Didn't you fellows leave some sort of a trail by which the police may find us?"

"No," Renny said.

Doc Savage had taken four more buttons off his coat, carefully unscrewed them, and emptied the contents on the cuff links. Try as he would, he could not reach the others. He waited. The radio in the next room had not been switched on. Silence was deep.

Once, Monk pondered aloud, "I wonder what happened to that girl?"

"And Leases Moore and Quince Randweil," Ham echoed.

IT must have been more than an hour later when voices became audible in one of the adjacent rooms.

"There's nothing more to hold us up," a voice said. "The balls are perfected to the point where they don't leave luminous trails at night, as did the first ones. We can go and come, and no one on earth can stop us."

Monk, in the intense darkness of the inner room, muttered, "So that's why there were streaks in the sky at first, but none any more."

"What about the prisoners?" a voice from outside queried.

"We'll get rid of them now."

Stunted's voice spoke up, saying, "I tell you jaspers, I don't like the idea of shootin' down anybody in cold blood."

"Aw, don't be a sissy!" he was advised.

The door had been locked. Now the fastenings rattled, and the panel opened. Men came in cautiously, spraying light from flashes. They cast the beams about.

"Look!" one of the men howled suddenly. He raced the white funnel of his flashlight. Stunned profanity came from those with him.

Doc Savage was missing from among the prisoners. The bronze man was not in the room.

Stunted ran over and howled at Monk, "How long has he been gone?"

"I dunno," Monk said, truthfully.

The man with the queer eyes dashed inside, heard what had happened, and snapped out a revolver. Stunted shoved against him heavily.

"Use your head!" Stunted snapped. "With these birds alive, Doc Savage will come fooling around, trying to get 'em loose. That way, we'll have a chance at him."

"You have got a brain, after all," growled the cross-eyed man, and pocketed his weapon.

The man went over to the spot where Doc Savage had been lying. He stooped, picked up a bit of metal, and examined it. The thing was a portion of a handcuff link.

The man touched a finger to it, then cried out in sudden pain and wiped the finger frantically on a handkerchief. He threw the handkerchief away.

"What is it?" Stunted demanded.

"Some powerful chemical of an acid nature," the man growled. "That infernal bronze fellow must have had it hidden somewhere on him, and put it on the handcuff chains. It weakened them until he could break them."

Stunted mumbled, "That's a new one on me."

Doc Savage could hear the voices—rather, hear the murmur of them, for he was not close enough to distinguish the words. He was in the gloom just outside the old ranch house. He had been free something like ten minutes, but had not left the vicinity for more than one reason. It was essential that he free the others. And he wanted a look at one of the fantastic ball conveyances.

There was one of the mysterious vehicles off to the right; its rounded hulk was vaguely distinguishable. Fog was making the night very dark. Doc eased toward the thing.

The size of the ball became more impressive as he drew close. He touched its smooth surface. It felt like glass. He moved around it, noting the polished nature of the covering, probably made thus to reduce friction. Even then, the heat generated must be tremendous.

He came finally to a door, barely large enough for him to wedge through. The door operated like a plug. The walls were thick—almost four feet, he judged.

Inside the thing, a small electric bulb glowed, furnishing illumination enough to get an idea of how the shell of the vehicle was constructed.

The outer surface, some compound resistant to friction and heat, no doubt, was only a skin, and under that was layer after layer of asbestos, interlaced with cooling pipes and wires and tubes and mysterious channels having to do with the operation of the contrivance.

The interior chamber was roughly circular, literally a bit of open space completely surrounded by machinery. There were devices on the walls, even the ceiling. Remarkable indeed was the fact that the control room seemed to have neither top nor bottom, as far as arrangement of the mechanism went. There were polished pipes, crisscrossing, their purpose hard to explain.

Doc examined the machinery. The first device he came to was an electrical mechanism for producing tremendous degrees of cold, a contrivance utilizing liquid air as its cooling element, in place of the more common ammonia.

This, then, was what kept the ball cool when in motion.

The liquid air-cooling device was a commercial product in part. Trademarks of the manufacturer were distinguishable. Doc read the plate.

REFRIGERATING, INC.
NEW YORK

The bronze man passed that up as not being of chief interest. How was this device propelled? What gave it the fantastic power to rip through space without benefit of propellers, or, as far as could be seen, rocketlike discharges.

Certain it was that the luminous exhaust which some of the balls exuded when in motion was not discharge of a rocket nature, as some had at first thought.

DOC SAVAGE began going over the largest and most intricate mass of apparatus. He had already gathered an infinite respect for the brain which had conceived all this. That respect became infinitely greater as he surveyed a set of huge motors which utilized a compressed gas as fuel. The things were of fabulous horse power for their size. There were, as far as Doc knew, no others like them in existence.

The exhaust of the motors explained the streams of sparks which some of the balls left. The burned gas came out of the exhaust in the form of flame. In this ball, the exhaust led through a digester which cooled it. Without the digester, the ball would leave a trail of the still-burning vapor.

The motors operated compact generators which undoubtedly delivered great voltage. Wires from the generators led into a metal-covered receptacle which undoubtedly held the secret of the whole incredible propulsion method. This was locked. Doc went to work on the locks.

He had operated only a moment when he heard voices outside. Men were approaching.

"We'll clear out of here before Doc Savage can come back with help," Stunted's voice said.

Doc's flake-gold eyes whipped about. Interior arrangement

of the ball was fabulously compact. Only a locker device to the left seemed to offer concealment. Doc lunged for it, got the metal door open.

The place had evidently been intended as a storage place for loot. It was empty, now, but yellowish marks on the rough metal showed where heavy gold bars had reposed—no doubt loot from the liner robbery in New York.

Doc closed the door. There were slits for ventilation, and through these he could look, if he were not discovered. He waited.

Men clambered up the narrow channel that led through the thick hull. The door was evidently heavy, for they closed it mechanically, then spent some moments with wrenches, connecting the pipes from the door to the cooling machine. Stunted was among them.

Under an arm, Stunted carried Monk's pet pig, Habeas Corpus. He had muzzled the porker to discourage biting tendencies.

"Let's go," Stunted said.

PROFUSE and strange experiences had come Doc Savage's way in the past, including many that bordered on the incredible, the fantastic. But this was one which was to stand out always in his memory.

His great metallic frame seemed to grow suddenly and mysteriously light. He lifted an arm instinctively, and the effort was incredibly easy. And once the arm was up, it did not drop back to his side. It seemed to possess no weight. The effort made him start a little, so that he lifted from the floor. He hung there, in mid-air. It was necessary to push himself back to the floor.

Out in the control room, things were happening which would have driven a superstitious person into a frenzy. Men were walking on the walls, the ceiling, adjusting the controls, and throwing switches.

The crisscrossing tubes, which had seemed so useless before, now advertised their use. They were hand rails, employed in going from one place to another. A man ran up one, spider fashion, body seeming to float in the air, then released his grip and floated where he was.

Doc Savage moistened his lips. He rarely showed excitement, but he was animated now.

Here before his eyes he was seeing demonstrated the product of a fantastic scientific discovery, a discovery so advanced that even the bronze man, for all of his learning, was somewhat dazed.

If he correctly interpreted what he was seeing, the creator of this aërial device had discovered how to nullify that type of force generally designated as momentum, as well as various forms of attraction, gravitational and otherwise.

No unschooled person could hardly have been more amazed than the bronze man. Here was inertia, gravitational attraction in all or most of its forms completely stifled. Some incredibly keen brain had penetrated one of the scientific fields probably least known to man. Modern science in general was not even quite sure what gravity was. Here was one who had mastered the subject.

The ball must be in motion. The machinery was making a great uproar. Shouted orders could not be heard. The men were communicating by gestures. One man in particular watched a bank of electric thermometers which registered the outer temperature of the shell and warned of increasing friction heat generated by their passage through the air. This man made a sudden gesture when the needles crept too high, and the speed of the ball was evidently slowed.

Other men glued eyes to periscope devices which evidently permitted them to look outside. Two more worked frantically with radio direction finders, evidently keeping track of their position by spotting well-known broadcasting stations on the earth below.

It was superscientific travel in its superlative degree, and Doc Savage could only stare and marvel. He was getting a vague idea of how the ball was made to move. No doubt gravitational force was nullified on top, on one side, creating in effect a vacuum in the lines of force which sucked the ball along.

It was a vague theory, capable of many refutations according to known scientific data, but it was the best solution the bronze man could assemble until such time as he had an opportunity to inspect the power plant itself.

The ball seemed to be arriving at its destination. Men made gestures. Others jerked levers, opened switches, and turned valves.

So completely was momentum nullified that even their stop, abrupt though it must have been, was not apparent. The noise of the mechanism ceased.

Doc Savage was conscious of an abrupt return of the normal heaviness of his limbs. He was conscious of something else, too—a terrific force which hauled him against the locker door, so that the door, unfastened as it was, fell open, and he came crashing out into the control room.

Too late, he understood what had occurred. The ball had stopped in a different position, so that the locker was now on what had become the ceiling. With the mechanism turned off, he had simply fallen out.

Chapter 14

OSAGE RENDEZVOUS

STUNTED saw the bronze man first. Stunted, knowing what would happen when the ball stopped, was holding to one of the crisscrossing bars. He let out a howl, dropped from his perch, and lunged for his sawed-off automatic rifle, which he had tied to a stanchion with a bit of stout cord.

"The devil himself!" Stunted bawled.

Two other men had gotten the hatch open and were making it fast. The opening was now on the side. They swung around, but were in a bad position to fight.

Doc lunged at Stunted. The latter was having trouble with the cord that held his rifle. He had used a cord too strong for him to break. He gave it up, retreated, and threw a wrench at Doc.

The bronze man dodged it, leaped upward and caught the crisscrossing bars. He made for the men at the hatch.

Doc was a master at this method of fighting. Where the others had to move slowly, supporting themselves, the bronze man whipped about with infinite agility. One man at the hatch dropped away. The other held his ground, maintaining a grip with one hand, trying to fend Doc off with the other.

That was a mistake. An instant later, he slammed heavily down on the metal plates beneath. A bronze, clublike fist had knocked him senseless.

From his vantage point under the hatch, Doc saw that he had a moment's respite before any of them would be in a position to use a gun. The bronze man was curious about where the ball had landed. He decided to look, and bobbed his head up.

What he saw changed his whole plan. He had intended to fight, overpower the men, take the ball, fathom its secrets. But he could never do that because, outside, there was a high concrete fence, and inside that, four other balls and something near two score of men. If the bronze man escaped, it would be a miracle.

A bullet smacked the rim of the hatch as he vaulted out. Stunted had gotten his rifle loose and fired it. The pig, Habeas, squealed shrilly.

Doc poised on the hatch edge, hanging by his fingers. There were men below, many of them. It was too dark for them to make out details, however.

Doc Savage exerted all of his powers of voice imitation and sent out a sharp, excited shout.

"Something's gone wrong!" he yelled. "This thing may blow up! Get away! Run!"

It was Stunted's voice which he imitated, and the shout held an edge of terror and warning which sent those below surging back.

Doc dropped down. The ruse would give him not more than a second or two. Less than that, it developed, for Stunted's real voice swore out from inside the ball, advising his fellows of the deception.

Doc ran for the wall. It was high, too high for him to leap. But it had been poured in a rough plank form, the planks stepped in toward the top for a narrowing effect. It could be climbed.

The bronze man leaped, caught hold, climbed, slipped, then gained the top just as a spotlight caught him and guns began crashing. He went over safely.

The other side, he discovered, was camouflaged with brush and transplanted vines. He carried some of the stuff with him as he went down. Then he ran. It was infinitely dark. He kept hands out before his face, in case he should run into something. Behind, they were organizing a pursuit party.

Then, to the left, a feminine voice called, "Over here, whoever you are!"

It was the girl, Lanca Jaxon.

Doc Savage found her a moment later. "We had better leave here," he told her.

"Oh, it's their big bronze trouble!" She sounded relieved. "You are supposed to be dead!"

"According to whom?" Doc asked.

"Leases Moore and Quince Randweil," she replied. "Listen to that uproar! We're going to have some trouble."

The shouting from inside the concrete compound had lost its confused note. A great many hand searchlights had appeared. Men were assembling outside the inclosure.

Doc found the girl's arm, and they began to work through the undergrowth. Timber here was thick, many of the trees large. Fallen logs made travel difficult.

"Three of the balls just arrived," said the girl. "I guess you were in one of them. Where are your men?"

"Prisoners," Doc said. "I suspect they are in the other balls."

"How did you get away?" she asked.

Doc told her, very briefly, making it sound rather simple, and finishing his recital with a question, "What are you doing here?"

"Leases Moore and Quince Randweil let me out of their ball," she replied. "They were afraid I would make trouble at the wrong time."

"Where do they hook into this?"

The girl laughed harshly, without humor. "They were slated for suckers."

Doc was ahead now, his superior agility and keener senses making for faster progress. Even at their best, they could hardly hope to distance those behind.

"The man who invented the balls got Leases Moore and Quince Randweil to finance him," said the girl, resuming. "Their idea was to do what they are doing: organize a gang and use the speedy balls for get-away vehicles in the commission of big robberies. But Leases Moore and Randweil were greedy. They demanded too big a cut. The gang grabbed them and held them. They were prisoners when you found them."

"And you?" Doc prompted.

Brush through which they traveled made *swishing* noises. There seemed to be no night birds. Evidently these had been frightened away by the arrival of the balls.

"They've been holding me out here for six months," the girl snapped. "I own this land around here. They're using it. And they've ordered all of the materials with which to build those balls, in my name, the idea being that I was the goat in case the law found out where the construction work had been done."

She gasped as a bough whipped her.

"It's too bad I didn't know who your two men, Monk and Ham, were when I tried to escape in that car yesterday," she said. "We might have gotten away. As it was, I ruined their break."

A bullet whistled through the branches, making sharp, ugly sounds, and the shot noise itself followed, thumping and echoing from the surrounding hills.

"This is the most deserted place in Oklahoma," the girl murmured. "Nobody will hear that shooting."

THE girl was breathing heavily now. She had fallen before, but she was falling more often now, and more heavily. She was slower getting up.

"I haven't slept for days," she said. "I guess I'm tuckered out."

Doc Savage picked her up, found what felt like a large tree, and moved out until, by jumping, he located a branch. With the grip of only one hand, and still carrying the girl, he swung up. He mounted with surprising speed.

"Take it easy," Lanca Jaxon said, uneasily. "This stuff might do on a circus trapeze, but I don't care for it here."

"We will wait here," Doc told her quietly. "If they miss us—excellent! If not, we'll try something else."

The bronze man waited, listening. With his free hand, he tested the dryness of the bark on the tree. Then he sniffed the air. It seemed that there had been a rain recently. That meant they had left footprints.

The rapidity and sureness with which their pursuers approached indicated they were following a trail.

"They'll come right to this tree," the girl breathed.

"Let me have your shoes," Doc requested.

She began, "Now, what——"

Doc whipped the shoes off her feet without more argument. Carrying them, he dropped downward and expended some moments locating the exact limb which he had seized from the ground in starting his climb. From there, he went on.

He used the girl's shoes, one in each hand, to make tracks beside his own footprints. Light and time for a finished job was lacking. He did the best haste permitted.

Men with searchlights and guns came up rapidly. They drew near the tree which held the girl. Just before they reached it, Doc grasped a dry limb and deliberately broke it. The cracking noise rattled through the timber.

"They're ahead!" Stunted roared, and the gang charged past the tree which held Lanca Jaxon, without dreaming of her close presence.

Doc found another tree and climbed it. He took a chance on the spreading boughs interlacing with other trees. They did. He went on. Reflected glow from the pursuing lights occasionally dashed palely among the treetops. Using that illumination, Doc picked the spreading limb of another tree, and with a tremendous swing through space, reached it. A professional gymnast would have been proud of that feat.

Shortly, the gang came upon the spot where Doc had gone aloft. They wasted much time probing the treetops, then spread out slowly, searching fruitlessly. But, by now, Doc was safely away.

The pursuers were persistent. It required fifteen minutes of hunting to disgust them, and then all did not favor giving up.

"Aw, we'll wait for daylight," advised the voice of the man with the uneasy eyes.

They turned back.

Aware that they might have left spies behind, Doc Savage was more than ordinarily cautious in returning to Lanca Jaxon. So silent was he that she gasped out sharply when he dropped to the limb beside her.

"They've given up!" she breathed. "When they passed under me, I thought sure——"

"I did not get to ask you the most important question of all," Doc told her. "Who is the individual behind all of this —the inventor of the balls?"

"I don't know for sure," she said.

"You have an idea?"

"That man with the shifting eyes," she said. "I have overheard things. If he is the big chief, not all of the gang know it."

"What did you overhear that led you to that idea?" Doc asked.

"The man with the crossing eyes was arranging with some of the others about murdering the one they call Stunted," she said. "He's to be killed whenever they have a chance to make it look like you did it."

"So they're going to kill Stunted," Doc murmured.

A moment later, the bronze man was gone into the darkness.

Doc Savage traveled swiftly, overtaking the party which was returning slowly toward the camouflaged compound which held the four weird ball craft, and the workshops where they had been manufactured.

The men were traveling without haste. All of them seemed to be tired. They walked around logs rather than over them, and their conversation was gloomy.

"This is sure a swell kettle of fish," Stunted said gloomily. "Right when we're set for a clean-up."

"Quit grousing!" snapped the man with the queer eyes.

Stunted stopped. He put out his jaw. His sawed-off automatic rifle shifted slightly under his arm.

"So you're still tryin' to push me around!" he gritted.

The other snapped, "Pipe down, you sawed-off runt!"

Stunted had ordinarily seemed a cheerful soul, inclined to keep control of his emotions even when aggravated to the point of desiring to shoot someone. But now he seemed changed. He glared. The gun moved under his arm; his hand dropped back to the trigger.

The other men saw the signs. They sprang forward, growling angrily, and got between Stunted and the man with the uneasy eyes.

"Cut it out, you two!" one ordered. "You're going to ride each other until one of you winds up picking lead out of himself!"

Stunted, glaring, said nothing. Shortly afterward, he permitted himself to be urged on ahead. Some of the group accompanied him. Others remained behind with the shifty-eyed man. These dropped well to the rear, and there was something deliberate about their behavior.

"We got a chance to talk now," one muttered. "Them guys ahead won't hear us. What're you gonna do about this bird Stunted?"

"I'll get him!" gritted the man with the roving eyes. "But I gotta be careful."

"Did you talk to the chief about disposing of Stunted?" a man asked.

"I did!" The other's eyes crossed and uncrossed evilly in the flashlight glare. "And what do you think?"

"What?"

"The chief said that if anything queer happened to Stunted, he'd croak me," gritted the conspirator.

"That's one for the book!"

"Uh-huh." The cross-eyed man turned his flash off. "It's kinda queer. Stunted seems plumb worthless to me. Him and his sawed-off automatic rifles! Blah!"

THEY were silent a while, listening, evidently to make sure no one was near, then they dropped their voices a little and began to discuss something which was obviously of greater importance.

"You found out for sure who the big chief is?" a man asked.

The one with the restless eyes cursed.

"No. He wears that mask all of the time. You know—that rubber hood of a business."

There was a meaningful pause.

"Our plan still goes, eh?" one growled.

"Sure." The uneasy-eyed man swore again. "We croak this head guy. We do it in a quiet way, see? Then we just tell the boys that I'm really the guy who invented the balls, and they won't know the difference. I'll get the chief's cut. You gents get yours."

"Swell!" said one. "When?"

"Soon as we can."

They went on, walking rapidly now, as if their tiredness was gone, overtaking the others.

Doc Savage clung to them like their own shadows. He had been close during the conference, and what he had heard was interesting, refuting as it did the girl's conviction that the man with the peculiar eyes was the actual mastermind.

They drew near the compound. A shrill, anxious challenge ripped out.

"Who is it?"

"Us," said the man with the uneasy eyes. "Retune that capacity alarm to compensate for our arrival."

Doc Savage heard that and moved even closer to the others in the darkness. One of the delicate capacity-balance alarms was in operation here, it seemed, and by adding or subtracting capacity at the controls, the operator managed to maintain a balance which would show the arrival of even a single man in the vicinity.

Doc's plan was to get close enough to the others that his own presence would be allowed for. He seemed to succeed.

The men filed through an opening in the high compound wall.

Doc did not follow them. That was too risky. The bronze man tackled the high wall, and covered by the noise of the others' arrival, managed to surmount it.

He lowered himself slowly down the other side, utilizing the indentations left in the concrete by the original plank forms.

Chapter 15

PLANS SINISTER

THERE was some faint light inside the compound. Men who had been working had moved over to the entrance—a gatelike affair flanked on one side by a building and on the other by a round tank. Evidently they were interested in how the search had come out, and being informed on that point, they scattered and busied themselves making the balls secure.

Doc Savage glided back through the shadows, reached one of the balls, and got under it, undiscovered. He was interested in getting inside, in examining the mechanism.

A stepladder evidently led up to the hatch. He climbed it, being careful that the ladder did not squeak. At the top, he explored with his fingers, but felt only the smooth, rounded, obsidian chillness of the hull. The hatch was there, its outlines barely traceable. But it was fastened, and there seemed to be no lock visible.

Feet scuffed the hard earth. Doc dropped from the ladder, scrambled behind the ball and crouched there. Men were approaching.

Stunted led them. The short man's chest was out and he looked pleased with himself. He came to the ball and climbed the ladder. Flashlights were turned on him.

From a pocket Stunted took what was unmistakably ordinary copper wires, a telegraph key and a battery, hooked in series. He touched the wires to two portions of the ball hull, where there were evidently contacts, held them there; then, covering the key with his coat so no one could see just what combination he tapped out, he manipulated the key.

The hatch was evidently operated by some electrical combination, for it opened. Stunted clambered inside, replacing his unique battery "key" inside his clothing.

He came out a moment later with a box larger than a suitcase. He handled this with great care. He passed it to those below.

"Watch it!" he snapped. "This is the heart of the invention.

Take that away and there ain't nobody can figure out how these balls work."

He descended the ladder, closed the hatch—which locked itself—then visited the other balls, and from each removed a similiar case of mechanism.

"What's the idea of taking these out?" he was asked.

"Don't we always do it?" Stunted demanded. "Supposin' that Doc Savage would get inside one of them balls? That'd be a swell howdy-do! We'll put these pieces of apparatus where we can watch 'em every minute."

Very gently, they carried the boxes to the large building beside the gate. All lights in the compound were now extinguished by way of precaution against being sighted by some nocturnal plane. They seemed surprisingly careless in the matter of a guard, too, evidently placing full dependence in the capacity alarm.

Doc Savage was not foolhardy enough to try to get into the building by the door. He moved to the right, felt along the rough concrete wall and found an open window.

An instant later, he was inside.

In the murk, a generator made shrill hum. Over to the left, something hot glowed. Doc studied it, and decided it was a forge with a banked fire.

Directly ahead, ranging along the side of the interior, was a partition perforated with doors, and some of these apertures were lighted. The men were toward the front.

Doc approached them. There was enough machinery to hide him—big drill presses, lathe beds, and other metalworking devices. Little expense had been spared in equipping the shop for the manufacture of the ball conveyances.

Stunted was saying loudly, "Everybody stay here and everybody stay awake. You can sleep later."

"What's up?" some one asked him.

"The chief is coming," Stunted said. "He told me to tell all of you that he wanted you on hand when he got here. He's gonna outline our next job, and it's to be bigger than anything we've pulled before."

"Since when did you become the chief's mouthpiece?" demanded the man with the shifting eyes.

Stunted grinned.

"Does it hurt?" he asked.

He was sworn at. Some one, evidently an admirer of Stunted, laughed. The man with the uncontrollable eyes got off by himself and mumbled.

Doc Savage eased closer. He was seeking his five aides and Spanner. A moment later, he saw them—all except Nock Spanner. Monk and Ham were tied together, probably because one of the gang had overheard them squabbling, and had mistaken their vocal hate as genuine.

Renny was by himself, trying to work his big fists through handcuff links. Long Tom and Johnny were barely discernible.

All five prisoners were in the room with the gang. Possibly twenty of the latter were present, every one armed. If Doc Savage had any impulse to charge in and attempt a rescue, he suppressed it carefully. He took chances, but never suicidal ones.

He moved back from the door as the lean man with the restless eyes came out of the lighted room, accompanied by two others. They lighted cigarettes, then strolled off.

"Stick around," Stunted called.

"We'll be in the radio room," one of the trio growled.

Doc Savage noted the direction they were taking—toward the monotonous hum of the generator. He put on speed himself, cutting in ahead of them, reaching the door of the room where the generator ran. He sought the corner by the door, and got down behind what was evidently a spare motor-generator unit.

The man with peculiar eyes came in. He cast a flash beam about.

"They're all with Stunted," one of the pair with him grunted.

"Watch the doors." The cross-eyed man went to the radio apparatus and turned on a light with a green shade. The radio was very modern. The man seemed to know a great deal about it, for he adjusted knobs and watched meters intently, then picked up a microphone.

The other two were at the door.

"No one coming," they advised.

Their leader's eyes crossed and uncrossed, and he spoke into the microphone, saying, "Hello—hello—hello," three times very rapidly, with pauses between, as if it were a signal.

Out of the loud-speaker came a lisping, hissing voice.

"How are things coming?" The voice made "things" sound like "thingsh."

"Slow," said the man with the roving eyes. "But we'll get the big shot to-night. He's due here before long, Stunted just said."

The lisping voice came over the radio again. Doc knew it;

he could not be mistaken. The speaker was Quince Randweil, who must be cruising the skies somewhere near by in the stolen ball.

"Leases and me just loaded a few hundred quarts of nitro," said Quince Randweil.

"What's the idea?" demanded the man at the radio.

"If it comes to that, we can blow that dump down there off the map," imparted Randweil. "Here's what we'll do if everything else fails: You and the guys working with you clear out and leave the others. Before you go, turn this radio transmitter on, and leave it turned on."

"I don't get this," said the man with the roving orbs.

"We'll use a direction finder on the radio," said Randweil. "That'll guide us to you. Then we'll use this nitro. That'll clean up the gang and wipe out their chief."

"But it'll mess up the balls," the other objected.

"We've got one." said Randweil, shortly. "That's enough. We can duplicate it if we have to."

"O. K.," agreed the man at the radio.

He laid down the microphone, switched off the apparatus, laughed once and walked out, followed by his two companions.

Doc Savage gave them time to join the others. He had plenty to think about to keep him from being impatient. These men were not conspiring alone, as it had at first seemed, but were associated with Leases Moore and Quince Randweil. Moore and Randweil, in turn, were proving more canny than hitherto.

Doc Savage left the radio room. He did not go too near the door beyond which the gang awaited—the room which held the prisoners. The bronze man stationed himself to the side of the gate, against the tank.

The tank was large, and smelled as if it held gasoline, possibly fuel for engines that ran the machine tools. The night had quieted down remarkably, and the cries of nocturnal birds had resumed.

There came a faint scraping from the gate.

A voice—it was the man with the peculiar eyes—demanded, "Who is it?"

"Me," said another voice shortly. "The chief."

There was a short scuffling sound, a blow, ugly but not loud, followed by a cry, a wispy, hideous thing that never really got started.

Doc Savage whipped from his cover, took half a dozen steps, then halted. Sane reason had told him he was late.

By the gate, a man laughed. The sound was strained. Some one lighted a cigarette.

A man put his head out of the workshop door and yelled, "Was that the chief?"

"Hell, no," said a man at the gate.

"Cut out the smoking," said the workshop voice. "Might be seen from the air."

"Sure, sure!"

The head withdrew into the workshop.

A moment later, Doc Savage heard three men coming from the gate toward the tank. They were infinitely furtive and walked as if burdened. Doc retreated slowly before them, and as they came around behind the tank, one displayed a flash beam cautiously.

It was the cross-eyed man and his two conspirators, and they carried the limp form of a fourth. The latter wore a long topcoat and a dark suit.

Seen in the flashlight glow, the limp individual's face was covered by a grotesque mask of flexible rubber; it could be seen plainly that the mask was padded so as to alter the apparent contour of the wearer's features.

"It's the big shot—the brains," the flashlight wielder grunted. "Let's have a look at that kisser of his."

They yanked off the rubber mask. Then they stared. They looked as if they were about to fall over. One dropped the flashlight.

The uncovered face was that of the girl, Lanca Jaxon.

Chapter 16

DEATH RODE THE SKY

THE cross-eyed man didn't hear Doc Savage coming, didn't dream of his near presence, probably never did know exactly what happened. His two companions knew. It helped them little, for there was not time to do anything about it.

They heard a jarring *thump*, and awakened from their surprise to see their chief collapsing under a tower of bronze. Then went for their guns. They carried the weapons in the open, in low-slung holsters, and old-time Western badmen could not have gone for them in more accepted style. One gun barely left its holster; the other stayed in the leather.

The two struggled a bit, madly. Their tongues ran out, and their faces purpled, even if they were not being choked. Nothing they did loosened the clutch on the backs of their necks, a grip of awful fingers which kneaded about as if searching for something down close to the spinal cords. After a while, the pair went limp.

Doc dropped them. He yanked the topcoat off the girl. The topcoat was big, loosely made, and Doc was just able to get into it. He picked up the mask. The rubber was of good quality, and it stretched. He got it down over his metallic features. He had some difficulty with the eyeholes.

The girl was limp when he picked her up. But there was life in her. She had been struck over the head, probably.

A man came out of the tool house. He was not excited.

"I heard something else," he said. "Was it the chief this time?"

Doc Savage stumbled toward him with the girl.

"Quick!" yelled the bronze man. "Doc Savage is in here!"

The other jumped as if a firecracker had gone off under his feet. He hit the ground with a gun in either hand, running. The fellow had nerve.

"Where'd he go?" he bawled.

Doc Savage was not using his normal voice, but a shrill, nondescript tone which might easily be mistaken for the unknown leader. He did not risk speaking now, but wheeled and leveled an arm toward the gate.

More men came out of the workshop, their wild exodus somehow remindful of the comic movies wherein a lion is discovered in a filled room. They saw Doc Savage, and since the bronze man was crouching to shorten his apparent stature, they mistook him for the mysterious leader whom they were awaiting. Doc's leveled arm sent them toward the gate.

"Where'd you get the girl?" one man yelled.

"She *was* with Savage," Doc said. And that was no lie.

Doc Savage looked into the room which held the prisoners. There were two men on guard, both pressing close to the one window, watching the pursuit conducted by their fellows.

The two were lax at the moment, whereas, a bit later, they would have been alert. But the moment was sufficient. Doc put the girl down, rushed them. They saw him just as he descended upon them. It was too late.

During the brief struggle, as the bronze man accomplished the by no means easy feat of holding a man with each hand and making them senseless simultaneously, Monk began to thrash about on the floor, and the pig, Habeas Corpus, came out of a corner, where he had been secreted.

Monk and his pet had recognized Doc.

WHEN the two men were unconscious, Doc lowered them. He leaped to the prisoners and began working on their bindings. He loosened their legs first. Wrists would have to wait, for they might need to move fast.

Monk got the gag out of his mouth. He was only handcuffed at the wrists, and hence could move his fingers.

"What happened?" he gulped.

"Help me loosen the others," Doc rapped.

Renny, ankles loosened, heaved erect.

"What do you think?" he boomed. "What do you think about that Nock Spanner?"

Monk growled. "Aw, you can't hardly blame Spanner."

"They promised Spanner that if he'd tell them what all we had learned about them, they'd turn him loose," Renny growled. "So he told them we hadn't learned much of anything, and they did turn him loose, back there in California, before they brought us here in them infernal balls."

"Spanner wanted to save his neck," Monk defended. "You can't blame him. That runt, Stunted, made the deal with Spanner. I think Stunted didn't want any more killing than was necessary. I think he got Spanner turned loose."

Ham got up and wrenched his gag out, then snapped, "I've been wondering if that Nock Spanner couldn't really be the chief of the gang?"

Doc Savage made no comment on that, a circumstance which caused Monk to look suddenly suspicious.

"Where did they put the apparatus that is the heart of those balls?" Doc asked.

"They've got a big iron safe in the next room," Monk explained. "Locked 'em up in there."

Doc Savage left the prisoners to free each other and lunged into the adjoining room. He found the safe. It was big, modern, and the lock was evidently similar to the electrical devices on the balls, for there was no knob visible.

The bronze man began to work at the door, seeking a method of opening it.

It was a baffling problem. He had no special tools. The vault was as burglarproof as science could devise.

Doc backed away and went into the workshop, searching for a cutting torch. There was almost certain to be one around. Eventually, he did locate one, but the tanks were disconnected and he had to assemble them, and the torch he had selected did not function properly.

He was working madly when two shots ripped out noisily and a man shouted, Doc lunged to the door. Three men had returned through the gate and discovered that something was wrong.

An instant later, Renny's big hand appeared in a window. It held a gun, evidently one taken from the guards. The gun went off four times so swiftly that it required a sharp ear to distinguish the reports.

One man fell down, then dragged himself out of sight, shot through the legs. The other two bounded back through the gate.

There was shouting from the woods. It did not come from very far away. The searchers were coming back. Against such a force—almost forty men—Doc and his group had little chance. The bronze man ran out into the open.

"We'll have to get out!" he shouted.

Renny bounded into view, still carrying the revolver. Long Tom, Johnny and Ham followed, supporting between them the girl, Lanca Jaxon, who seemed to be regaining consciousness. Monk did not appear.

"Monk!" Doc called.

There was a pause and no answer.

"*Monk!*" Doc made it louder.

The homely chemist popped through the door. He had his pig.

He gulped, "If I only had a minute or two more——"

"Come on!" Doc clipped.

THEY did not run for the gate. The men outside would make exit by that route difficult. They moved back to the rear, and climbed the wall. Doc assisted in getting the girl up and over. She was able to help herself a little. Five revolver bullets made the final stages of their climb exciting.

Going down the other side, they carried much of the camouflaging along. Renny produced a flashlight.

"Found it on the floor!" he boomed. "It's sure gonna help!"

"It will," Doc agreed. "It may save our lives."

They used the flashlight as little as possible at first, not wishing to draw more bullets.

The girl dropped alongside of Doc Savage. She fell down frequently. Her voice was hoarse.

"I made a bad move," she said. "I got tired of waiting in that tree. I was worried about you."

Doc advised, "You should have stayed there."

"I know it." She took a header, got up at once. "I climbed out of the tree and went toward the compound, and pretty soon I heard some one. He used a flashlight and I saw it was their chief, wearing his rubber mask. So I got a stick and clubbed him."

"Kill him?" Doc asked.

She gasped out, "No! He was still alive! I felt of his pulse."

Doc queried, "Then what?"

"I put on his regalia," she said swiftly. "I thought maybe I could get in and help you, or free some of the other prisoners before they got wise. I can make my voice hoarse. Listen."

She made her voice hoarse, and it sounded almost masculine as she continued, "I got as far as the gate, and was coming in when some one must have struck me down."

"I saw that part," Doc told her.

She sobbed once.

"I've made an awful mess," she wailed. "I've got men killed and everything."

"Got men killed?"

"Two of them," she elaborated. "The first was one of the gang, whom I bribed to send a message to Willard Spanner. You see, I knew Willard Spanner, and knew that he was a friend of yours, and I wanted you on this affair, and thought I'd get you through Spanner."

"So that's how it was." Doc helped her. Pursuit was overtaking them.

"They must have spied on the man who took the message, made him tell about it, then killed him," she said. "Then they killed Spanner, first seizing him in San Francisco, then taking him to New York and making him get a letter telling the whole story, which he had mailed to his New York address, in case anything happened to him. He marked the envelope so it would be turned over to the police if he did not appear to claim it. I heard them talking about it."

Monk howled, "We're gonna have to travel faster than this."

Doc Savage stopped very suddenly. "Listen!"
They halted.
"I heard it, too," Monk muttered.

Chapter 17
HOLOCAUST

"It" was a faint moan of a noise, and seemed to come out
of the sky far above, persisting only a moment before it died
away.

Doc Savage, listening, made a faint, exotic trilling noise, a
sound which he made under profound emotion, surprise,
sometimes puzzlement. It was an indistinct tone, eerie in
quality, and covering a large range. Then, with a snapping
leap, he was at Monk's side.

"What's wrong?" Monk gulped.

"What were you doing back there when we called you?"
Doc rapped.

"Why—uh—I was in their radio room." The imperative
tone of Doc's demand had taken the homely chemist's breath.

"Why?" Doc barked.

Monk let his pet pig fall. Something was up.

"Uh—I thought I'd send out an SOS," he explained.
"Somebody might have picked it up and notified the cops.
We need all of the help we can get. I intended to tell you
about it."

"Did you leave the transmitter on?" Doc queried with a
studied calm.

"Sure. Why?"

It was a long moment before the bronze man answered,
and during that interim, it was noticeable that sounds of pursuit had ceased, indicating those behind had also heard the
moaning sound in the night sky and correctly interpreted its
meaning.

"Leases Moore and Quince Randweil had an arrangement
with their friends in the gang to drop nitroglycerine on that
inclosure if the radio was turned on and left on," Doc said.

Monk said cheerfully, "Well, that oughta wipe the place
off the map. Good riddance, I'd call it!"

But Doc Savage seemed to have other ideas. He listened. Shouting of their pursuers was faintly audible.

"Leases Moore and Quince Randweil are above us in their ball!" a man yelled. "We'd better get back to the pen."

"Sure!" barked another. "We'll rig our own balls! It'll be daylight soon. Then we'll chase this Doc Savage in the balls and use gas on him. We may be able to spot Moore and Randweil, too."

Doc Savage left his own group suddenly, and went toward the pursuers. He moved swiftly. Sounds told him they were going back.

"You fellows!" he called sharply.

They stopped. Silence held them. Then one shouted suspiciously.

"Whatcha want?"

"This is Doc Savage," Doc told them.

"We know that voice," one barked. "Whatcha want?"

Doc hesitated. He had faced this problem before—whether to guarantee his own safety and the safety of his friends by permitting others to die. But it was against his policy, a policy to which he adhered rigidly, to see human life taken needlessly if there was any possible method of avoidance. He reached the decision he had known he would reach.

"Do not go back to that compound," he shouted. "Leases Moore and Quince Randweil may drop nitroglycerine on it!"

Stunned silence fell over the darkened timberland.

THE quiet held for some moments, and toward the end of the interval, Doc was not looking at the spot where the foes stood in the darkness, but at the sky above the compound.

The compound was lighted brilliantly now, illumination having been switched on during the excitement. The lights were very bright. They threw a glow upward some distance.

A gleaming object was outlined above the compound. It poised there, bobbing up and down a little, its presence marked only by the vague rays from below. The ball vehicle of Leases Moore and Quince Randweil!

"It's a trick!" a man shrilled. "The bronze guy is trying to keep us away from the pen!"

They ran back, and although Doc Savage called out again, it had no effect. Doc fell silent, and stood there, unpleasant expectancy gripping him.

Renny came up, splashing a flashlight beam.

"Didn't do much good," he said dryly.

Doc made no reply; the others of his party gathered nearer. The ball was still above the compound, swaying up and down, as if the control device was not perfected to a point where the thing could be held absolutely stationary.

Then a rifle smacked. Others followed. A machine gun made rapid stuttering sounds.

From within the compound, they were shooting at the ball, striving to drive it away. The gunfire became a continuous volley.

Suddenly, a round spot of light appeared on the undersurface of the ball. A port had been opened.

Below the ball, dropping swiftly, came something small and black. It fell lazily. In size, it was like a beer keg. Another of the articles appeared, then a third—a fourth—a fifth. All five of them were in the air—when the first hit the ground.

The world turned blasting white as the nitroglycerine struck, and the earth heaved and tumbled and trees fell over. Bushes lost their leaves. The wind of the explosion, reaching as far as where Doc and his party stood, upset them, and the ground, shaking, tossed them about as if in an earthquake.

From the compound, there was no screaming. Possibly no man lived to scream after the blasts. Flame and débris were in the sky, and the ball, fantastic thing that it was, had backed up into dark nothingness until it was now invisible.

Débris falling back, made a great roar; it added more fuel to the flaming compound, and slavering copious quantities of black smoke kited upward.

"The gasoline tank!" Lanca Jaxon said hoarsely.

After that, no one said anything.

The balls in the compound had been shattered. They could not see them. The smoke spread, mushrooming, and the light of the flames jumped above it and played like scarlet goblins on a black toadstool.

Doc said, "We had better see if we can do something."

But before they could move there came a sobbing noise from above, as of a gigantic bat in swift passage, and the ball of Moore and Randweil was suddenly above them.

"They're gonna attack us!" Monk shouted.

THEY were standing in an open space, plainly lighted by the flames. They had been seen. Doc sent out an arm, and started them for the cover of the nearest tree. The girl was past running swiftly, and he carried her.

As soon as they were under the foliage, such of it as still

stuck to the trees, the bronze man urged them sharply to the left. Fallen limbs were thick on the ground.

"Get down under this stuff and crawl," Doc directed.

They did that. A minute passed. Two. Then the earth heaved under them, a fabulous crash set their eardrums ringing, and there was white fire in the air, as if lightning had struck. Débris fell all about, making sounds like fast running animals.

"Nitro!" Renny howled. "They're trying to finish us!"

The branches under which they lay had shifted a little, and Doc Savage, looking up, could see the ball, the open hatch like a round, evil red eye. It bobbed toward them, something hideous and incredible in its movement. They could hear the noise of machinery inside.

A man had head and shoulders over the hatch opening. He was a plump, rounded man—Quince Randweil, no doubt, and he was looking down. They could see him waving an arm behind his back. He had seen them, was directing Leases Moore, at the controls, to bring the ball directly over them.

Then Quince Randweil drew back for a moment, and when he showed himself again, he was gripping a container of nitro as large as a beer keg. He had some difficulty holding it, and, leaning down, made ready to drop it.

Monk said in a dry, shrill voice, "Ham, if we're gonna die now, I want to apologize for riding you."

Ham mumbled, "You big ape——"

Doc Savage rapped, "Renny! That revolver you are——"

A revolver went *bang!* beside them. There was a louder report overhead, so infinitely much louder that it beggared description.

Doc Savage, who was looking directly at the ball and Randweil, knew the nitro Randweil held had exploded. One instant the ball was there; the next it was not—and the bronze man's eyes held only pain, and knowledge of terrible danger from exploding parts of the aërial vehicle.

He did not know how long afterward it was that some one spoke. It was Renny's voice.

"I didn't intend to do that," Renny said.

He was shifting his revolver from one hand to another, as if it were hot. He looked at Doc.

"What else could I do?" he mumbled.

"Nothing," Doc told him.

"I didn't intend to hit the nitro," Renny groaned. "Honest, I didn't. I figured on shooting past that Randweil bird and scaring him into dropping the stuff before he reached us. But no man can shoot straight in this light."

"You didn't do bad," said Monk, who was inclined to be the bloodthirsty member of Doc's crowd.

"No man can shoot straight in light like this," Renny grumbled again. "I should've let Doc do it. You were asking for the gun just as I shot, weren't you, Doc?"

"Yes," said the bronze man. "Come on. Let us see what we can do at the compound."

THEY could do nothing. That was evident when they came close. The blast of the nitro had been terrific, and had shattered, not only the four balls, but the workshop and the tank as well.

One missile must have landed directly on the workshop—possibly more; for hardly a trace of the place remained other than twisted steel and blasted woodwork. Even the compound walls had been broken into surprisingly small pieces.

Doc Savage gave particular attention to where the safe had been. Hope that it had survived faded, for he distinguished one side and back standing where the flames were hottest. The floor of the workshop had been low, and the ruptured gasoline tank had poured its contents into the depression.

There was no hope that the "hearts" of the weird aërial balls, the mechanism which was the secret of their amazing performance had survived.

"Holy cow!" Renny said gloomily. "It looks like nobody is ever gonna know how them things worked."

Doc Savage nodded slowly. He would investigate, of course, but it was doubtful if the secret could be solved. Some new theory must have been stumbled upon, by accident. But he would work on it, work hard for the next few months, he resolved.

Monk took his eyes from the flames and looked pained, as if something had just stung him.

"We should have thought of it before!" he exploded.

"What?" Renny boomed.

"Lanca Jaxon, here, knocked out the mastermind, the bird who invented these balls," Monk explained. "She said she left him unconscious. Maybe he's around somewhere. If so, we can grab him and make him tell——"

"No use," Lanca Jaxon said, hoarsely.

"Why?" Monk eyed her, puzzled.

"I left him close to the compound wall," she said. "He was killed with the rest. I am sure of it."

Monk returned to gloomy depths, but almost at once started again, seized by another thought.

"Who did you knock senseless?" he asked.

"Stunted," said the girl. "That runty fellow—Stunted."

Renny made some comment that had to do with the way things had come out. His voice was a throaty roaring as Doc Savage listened to it.

It might have been a forewarning of what the future held.

But Renny, not having been gifted with the ability to fathom what the future held, went on with his roaring-voiced conversation.

OUT OF THIS WORLD!

That's the only way to describe Bantam's great series of science-fiction classics. These space-age thrillers are filled with terror, fancy and adventure and written by America's most renowned writers of science fiction. Welcome to outer space and have a good trip!

☐	THE MARTIAN CHRONICLES by Ray Bradbury	2440	$1.75
☐	STAR TREK: THE NEW VOYAGES by Culbreath & Marshak	2719	$1.75
☐	THE MYSTERIOUS ISLAND by Jules Verne	2872	$1.25
☐	ALAS, BABYLON by Pat Frank	2923	$1.75
☐	FANTASTIC VOYAGE by Isaac Asimov	2937	$1.50
☐	A CANTICLE FOR LEBOWITZ by Walter Miller, Jr.	2973	$1.75
☐	HELLSTROM'S HIVE by Frank Herbert	8276	$1.50
☐	DHALGREN by Samuel R. Delany	8554	$1.95
☐	STAR TREK XI by James Blish	8717	$1.25
☐	THE DAY OF THE DRONES by A. M. Lightner	10057	$1.25
☐	THE FARTHEST SHORE by Ursula LeGuin	10131	$1.75
☐	THE TOMBS OF ATUAN by Ursula LeGuin	10132	$1.75
☐	A WIZARD OF EARTHSEA by Ursula LeGuin	10135	$1.75
☐	20,000 LEAGUES UNDER THE SEA by Jules Verne	10325	$1.25

Buy them at your local bookstore or use this handy coupon for ordering:

DOC SAVAGE

To the world at large, Doc Savage is a strange, mysterious figure of glistening bronze skin and golden eyes. To his fans he is the greatest adventure hero of all time, whose fantastic exploits are unequaled for hair-raising thrills, breathtaking escapes, blood-curdling excitement!

Bantam Book Catalog

Here's your up-to-the-minute listing of every book currently available from Bantam.

This easy-to-use catalog is divided into categories and contains over 1400 titles by your favorite authors.

So don't delay—take advantage of this special opportunity to increase your reading pleasure.

Just send us your name and address and 25¢ (to help defray postage and handling costs).